A Riff on the Blues

M Roy Duffield

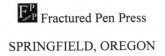 Fractured Pen Press

SPRINGFIELD, OREGON

Michael Duffield/Fractured Pen Press
Springfield, Oregon 97478
www.website-url.com

Publisher's Note: This is a work of fiction. Names, characters, places, and incidents are a product of the author's imagination. Locales and public names are sometimes used for atmospheric purposes. Any resemblance to actual people, living or dead, or to businesses, companies, events, institutions, or locales is completely coincidental.

Book Layout © 2014 BookDesignTemplates.com

Cover photos © 2015 MRDuffield/Fractured Pen Press

A Riff on the Blues/M Roy Duffield. -- 1st ed.
ISBN 978-0-9968061-0-7

This book is dedicated to my best friend, Ruth, who is also my wife. And to my children who have endured a distracted father for far too long.

The universal line of distinction between the strong and the weak is that one persists; the other hesitates, falters, trifles, and at last collapses or "caves in."

—EDWIN PERCY WHIPPLE (1819-1886). "Character," 1857, *Character and characteristic men,* 1884

Jeffrey Grant heard a car door slam. An engine started and the car accelerated away. In the distance he saw a pair of red tail lights turn the corner. The sound faded into the night.

His steps resonated on the damp sidewalk. Jeffrey enjoyed the late night walk home from the Newsome Hotel. After playing a five hour gig it was good to be outdoors. The cool breeze was refreshing. By the time he got home, he would be tired but relaxed.

The weather determined the route he would take home, direct in a downpour, roundabout in a light drizzle. Tonight Jeffrey took the long way home. The scenery along the university grounds shone eerie in the light of the lamps along the path. Sounds of scrabbling squirrels in the trees and crickets turning on and off in the distance punctuated the orchestra that was his theme song as he strolled, lost in his thoughts.

He ran the melody of "Take Five" through his head and imagined playing variations on a sixteen bar solo. He could feel his fingers walk down the frets and moved fluidly along with the five four beat. It was the last song of the night. It was always the last song.

He tugged his jacket tighter. The nicotine gum he was chewing had lost its bite and it tasted like a wet eraser. It was time to get rid of it. Since 9/11, finding an outdoor wastebasket had become a challenge.

He saw an opening in the hedge that led to a university building. A trash can sat at the bottom of the steps. A single light protruded from the left jam of the entrance. The light was stuck like a carbuncle to the frame, a florescent plastic fixture with a blue-white light. The sidewalk to the building was unlit, dark.

He felt a chill and pulled his jacket tighter. As he walked to the wastebasket he became aware of the silence. He tossed his gum in it, glad to be done with it, ready to get back to the street. Ominous conjunctions of shadowy shapes melted into the steps and side of the building. A cricket chirruped and a squirrel clicked along the branch of a tree in the darkness.

Out of the corner of his eye Jeffrey spotted a shoe between the trash bin and hedge. It rested at an odd angle near the bin. He stepped near it and leaned over. It was a sneaker, he kicked at it. It barely moved. It was attached to an ankle wearing black socks and a leg clad in slacks that protruded from the hedge.

"Sorry about that," he said into the hedge. "Are you okay?"

The odor of damp earth drifted up to his nostrils. It smelled as though the ground had been recently disturbed. The crickets stopped. Jeffrey waited. Then he squeezed between the hedge and the metal banister at the base of the steps. Moving blindly, he slid his feet along wet grass hoping not to step on what he assumed was a student passed out from a rough night.

"Hello?" he said into the dark.

He slid his feet along the grass until he felt an object. He wrestled a lighter out of his jacket pocket. The flame bounced and the light didn't help much. He could make out a black shape on the ground. He leaned over and brushed his foot against the body. He expected to hear a snore or heavy breathing, but the only sound was the night. The flame went out. Drops of water clicked down leaves in the hedge as he waited, the sound magnified by the silence. Re-striking the lighter he brought the flame closer to the ground. Jeffrey saw a tangle of black hair and a dark jacket, the face was turned down into the grass. There was no breath, no movement. Their arms pushed alongside the body, one leg jammed through the hedge, the other splayed awkwardly to the side. He touched a shoulder and shook it.

"Hello," he said. A chill ran along his spine when he touched the body. Even shaking the shoulder he felt an unexpected resistance in his hand.

Dead? It was a dead man, not drunk, not passed out. Now what? He felt a pain begin to burn in his stomach. His throat constricted. He tugged his cell phone out of his jacket and dialed nine-one-one. As the call connected time became warped, his sense of panic morphed into confusion.

The voice on the phone asked questions. He replied mechanically and was told to wait until someone arrived. What else could he do? He pushed back through the hedge to the sidewalk. He was alone. The glow of light from the building looked brighter than before. The beam cast an eerie blue layer of light on everything. Jeffrey felt tired. Without thinking, he slowly walked out to the street.

The mist turned into a drizzle. Pockets of water formed on the sidewalk. Punctuated by raindrops that hit the puddles, a minor symphony began to play as the night wore on.

CHAPTER TWO

The wail of sirens grew. Jeffrey didn't want to jump to conclusions but the person didn't look alive. He should have done CPR, maybe the kid had taken drugs. The siren grew closer, an echo kicked off the nearby brick building, cacophony broke out as flashing lights grew larger. Rudely, the flashing lights of the patrol car lit up the area.

Other sirens began to rise in the distance. A flashlight shone into his eyes.

"You made the call?" the officer asked.

Jeffrey explained what happened. The officer checked out the body then made some calls.

Another officer arrived and pulled Jeffrey aside. Jeffrey answered questions. Flashlights whipped around by the building, he heard the crackling of police radios. The blast of a horn said a fire truck arrived.

A detective arrived and introduced himself as John Madison. He wore a dark t-shirt with the logo of North Glendon on it. Over that was a jacket with his name and rank. He had dark circles around his eyes. He sat Jeffrey into the back of a patrol car and Madison went to speak with the patrolmen. Eventually he came back to talk with Jeffrey.

"How is it that you found the body?" asked Detective Madison.

"I'm on my way home," said Jeffrey. "I play in the nightclub at the Newsome downtown."

"Newsome Hotel," said the detective. He scratched into a notebook. "So why did you go back by the building?"

"I saw the trash can down there and stopped to toss out my gum. The shoe was sticking out. I touched it with my foot thinking it was an odd place for leaving sneakers."

They went through question and answer for a while. Then Madison decided he had enough information. He walked over to talk with two people in suits who were gathering evidence in bags. By now yellow tape circled the crime scene and a police van had arrived. At the ambulance two men were pulling a stretcher out of the back. Madison returned and told Jeffrey he was free to go.

That night Jeffrey stared at the ceiling. He was tired but couldn't sleep. He texted 'r u awake' then waited for a reply. A minute later his phone chirped. 'Now I am.' He sent back, 'Meet me at breakfast the usual place.'

Dawn arrived with a mix of gray clouds and slashes of yellow blue light that fell through the open blinds. Jeffrey awoke feeling exhausted and sluggish. There was a message on his phone. It was Detective Madison requesting an interview with him at the police station. He called back after several cups of coffee.

"Madison here," said the detective.

"This is Jeffrey Grant. You left a message that I should call," said Jeffrey.

"Thanks for returning my call Mr. Grant. I've got a few more questions I need to ask you. When can you be here?"

"Can't I answer them over the phone?"

"I'd prefer you come here. Ten o'clock would be good."

"All right then, ten,"

"Tell the desk sergeant to call me when you get here." Madison hung up.

Bill Clemons waited for Jeffrey at a back table in the Riverside Cafe. Up high on several walls were monitors tuned to the morning news. Of the half dozen busy tables, most of the patrons were either watching or glancing up to see the latest on the screens. Silverware on ceramic plates created a discordant symphony of sound punctuated by the barking of orders and the din of conversation that breathed through the room like a minor whirlwind moving from table to table. Two plates with omelets, toast and bacon waited. The waiter poured coffee just as Jeffrey walked up.

"Thanks, Gary," said Bill.

"The usual?" said Jeffrey.

"It's always good to me. You look tired."

"See the paper yet?"

"I haven't read a paper in years."

"I'm on the front page." Jeffrey ran his hand across his face. "I found a body on the way home last night."

"No joke?"

"No. I've been up most of the night. Police interviewed me. I've had no sleep. I tried but I kept seeing images of the body on the ground."

"Know who it is?"

"No. He had dark hair and dark clothing."

"Are you alright?"

"I'm going in to the police to answer more questions when we're done here. You know it's not like it looks on TV. I feel like I've been slapped around. Beat up. I just ache all over. My head hurts like I'm hung over."

"Who do you think it is?"

Jeffrey leaned over. "You don't understand. The police think I was the last one to see the man who died. They're going to check up on me."

"So?"

"I can't have them look into my background."

"Why?"

"I can't."

"Okay."

Outside a breeze had picked up. The light fog that rolled in overnight hadn't settled for long. As pockets of moisture drifted away and the morning began to warm up, the sound of car engines and general activity began to punch its way into town. Jeffrey and Bill left the Riverside Cafe.

A high school marching band could parade up the steps to the city government offices. At the top of the rise stood a plaza that led to the buildings used by the elected officials of the city North Glendon. Streaks of morning sunlight filtered through the green and brown hues of the plants that lined the plaza walls. It created a setting like a small forest.

Detective John Madison walked through the forest. In his late fifties, Madison carried a cup of java in one hand and a newspaper tucked under his arm. In his other hand he carried a battered brown briefcase. The brown in his close-cropped hair was streaked with gray. He wore a nondescript blue suit that fit well enough. He ignored the drizzle that had been falling all morning and walked to his office.

Inside the offices of the Police Department of North Glendon, officers and office workers jostled through entrances and exits. The smell of cleaning solutions mixed with paint and waxed floors permeated the building. Today the business of the Police Department was ramping up slowly.

Madison went to his office. It was back in the cubicles that lined the far corner of the room. Wilson DeBrough and Jason Korman, fellow detectives, arrived at their own cubicles.

"Morning to both of you," Madison said.

"Yes, it is," said DeBrough. He dropped a briefcase on his desk. Younger than John Madison by fifteen years, he had already put in a solid ten years as a detective.

"Looks like you've got plenty to do on your new case," Korman said. He tossed a gym bag into the corner then dropped himself into a desk chair. His football days were well behind him and his tall frame had become overweight from lack of exercise and too much comfort food.

"Looks like you're tagged to run-down interviews for me. By the way the Chief didn't like the headline today," said Madison. "I got that message on the way in."

"So, what does it look like to you? Are you thinking she died from natural causes or homicide?" said DeBrough.

"Too soon to know, papers guess natural causes. I'll wait for the ME report and take it from there," said Madison. His phone rang.

CHAPTER THREE

At the front desk of the police department Jeffrey asked for the detective. The clerk directed him to a phone bank and Jeffrey dialed an extension. A short time later Madison arrived and they went into an interview room.

"Mr. Grant I've got a few questions about the incident last night at the university."

"I just found that guy laid out. I thought he was drunk." Jeffrey said.

"It was a she. She was dead."

"Oh."

"I'm going to go over some of the questions from last night. You said you were walking home from the Newsome Hotel. You work in the Jazz Room?"

"Right. I sometimes walk that way," he said.

"Did you see anyone or notice anything unusual?"

"Aside from her body?"

"Aside from her body."

"No."

"Do you know Sharon De LaFleur?" he asked.

"From the Newsome? She's one of the waiters. That Sharon?"

"You knew her then?" Madison asked.

"Yes, she works the bar in the Jazz Room. We would talk at times. Was that was her?"

"According to the pocketbook we found. Yes."

Jeffrey blanched. A wave of nausea washed over him. He leaned over and put his hands on his face.

"Just a few more questions, okay?"

"Yeah, sure."

"You were friends with her?"

"Just from work."

"Did you know anything about her personal life?"

"Not really. She seemed nice, she was studying at the university. Psychology, I think. I saw her last night as we wrapped up the gig."

"Did you spend time with her outside of work?"

"No."

Jeffrey fidgeted in his chair. They suspected him. He was the person who found her. He knew her from work. He admitted seeing her that night.

Madison watched Jeffrey piece together his thoughts.

"How well did you know her? Were you intimate with her?"

"No. We went out a few times, but didn't click."

"Why not?"

"She was nice, but too quiet. It seemed like she was not really in the moment. You know?"

"You mean, distant or preoccupied?"

"Preoccupied. Not enjoying the moment."

"You're older than she was?"

"Not that much, maybe ten or fifteen years. What does that mean?" Jeffrey began to rise out of his seat.

Madison stood up and waited until Jeffrey sat down again.

"So you weren't intimate?"

Jeffrey slammed his hand on the table. "I told you, no. We never had sex."

"What about her friends at the Newsome. Did she have a boyfriend or a confidant?"

"How would I know? I'm just a guitar player. I'd see her at night sometimes. Go ask them yourself."

"We are talking to them. Did you notice Sharon arguing with anyone recently?"

"I told you I didn't see her much."

"Okay. I think that's all for now. Keep yourself available. Let me know if you recall anything odd about last night. Here's my card."

Madison stood up. Jeffrey was free to leave.

A call downstairs told Madison the crime scene pictures were still being printed, he would have them by eleven. He called the ME's office. The autopsy was starting in an hour.

Dr. Janet Winslow, North Glendon's Medical Examiner, had already begun by the time Madison arrived. The body of Sharon De LaFleur was being photographed by an assistant. Winslow supervised. She invited Madison to join them.

"Doc," he said.

"Madison. You've got an interesting case here. She has lots of debris from the ground. She has abrasions along her arms, but I don't know from what. Once we get her clothes off I'll know more."

"Has she been formally ID'd?"

"No. We're still going with the purse found at the scene for now. The drivers' license matches."

"Good."

"Did you notice the earrings?"

"No. I didn't move her last night. The techs did their stuff and I only got a quick look at the body before they picked her up."

"You wouldn't have seen them. They weren't there."

Two hours later Madison made an excuse to leave, the autopsy would continue without him.

Back at the office he took another look at the incident report. The victim was noted as Sharon Carolyn De LaFleur, twenty-four, five feet six inches tall, one hundred eighteen pounds, brown hair, and brown eyes. Her address was not far from the university. The list of items found with the body was short. Earrings were not among them.

Madison requested a background check on De LaFleur. It was early in the case, but the interview with Jeffrey Grant didn't seem right. Something was missing. Usually the last person with the victim was the perp. Madison wondered if Jeffreys' anger during the interview was real or not.

When the background check came through there was not a lot of information to go on. No known alias, no criminal record, several local addresses within the last five years, currently part time employee of the Newsome Hotel and university student. He would have the addresses checked out and take a trip to the university himself.

At the end of the day Madison read through the preliminary autopsy report. Dr. Winslow hadn't found a cause of death. Further tests would be forthcoming. Trace evidence found on the body was consistent with the crime scene; there was no reason to believe the body had been moved. The report also said there was no evidence of sexual activity, although swabs had been taken and results would be in the final report. While there were no indications of drug use, the ME believed the tox report would pinpoint the cause of death as was often the case in these circumstances. One further note was that several tattoos had been found and were included in the photos filed with the report.

Officer James Minor's crime scene report backed up what the ME stated, De LaFleur's identification was made by her driver's license, found in her pants pocket. Trace evidence from the scene had been sent to the lab. He put down the report. If the newspaper was right and she had killed herself, then this was an odd way to go about it. Why hidden behind a bush at the university? What would have driven De LaFleur to commit suicide?

Chapter Four

I t was Sunday night after the body had been found. A campus security guard, Carolyn Pendle, was called about a student fight near the apartments. She was on her way.

A squawk came out of the thin man's mouth. His body wavered as he raised his fists like a boxer. Nearby, sitting on the pointed dome of a garden gnome, sat an overweight man in running shorts and a t-shirt. His belly leaked out between the shirt and over his shorts. His head bobbled around, his eyes closed, his arms lax at his side.

"You're drunk," yelled the woman on the front steps of the house. She threw a sandal at the men.

"Get back in here before security comes, you idiot."

"Neither of them can even see anymore," said the woman next to her. She was holding two beers, giggling.

The thin man let out a liquid burp and staggered toward the big man.

Students filtered out from adjacent houses hoping to witness a fight. A few recorded the events on their cell phones. In this university neighborhood, any activity, loud, rude, or stupid, would draw a crowd.

The thin man landed a punch into the back of the other man then fell to his knees.

"I'm not hauling you in here like before," she said.

"Looks like security is here," said one of the onlookers. The words University Security glowed under the street light as the golf cart approached.

Upright once more, the thin man wavered. He propelled himself toward the other man. The two of them tumbled together and backwards. Malleable bodies hit the driveway in a squishy thud, the big man screamed like a little girl and the thin man barfed onto both of them.

Sounds of disgust mingled with rude exclamations. Laughter rippled, heads shook. Like a crowd at a tennis match, they turned in unison to the security guard and watched her stride across the lawn. The radio crackled at her hip.

Carolyn Pendle approached as the thin man rose. He lunged and in one swift move she grabbed his wrist, turned him around, and brought out her plastic cuffs. This wasn't the first time she had dealt with these two. His wrists cuffed, he moaned as she rose and left him.

Flatulence echoed in the night. Collectively, the crowd stepped back. Carolyn pulled gloves from her pocket, slipped them on, then rolled the other man up. He abruptly propelled himself up on one leg and swung his arm around. Carolyn ducked away from his fist, slipped a foot behind his, and stiff-armed him in the chest.

"Stupid cow!" said the woman who had spoken earlier. "You're done."

"Get up and get out or I'm making the call so you can sober up in a holding cell," Carolyn said. She flipped out her flashlight and focused on his face. She saw blood, decided the injury was superficial. She walked over to the thin guy. He groaned when he saw Carolyn, his eyes fully open. She directed the flashlight into his eyes.

"Okay," he said. He flailed his arms out on the driveway and exhaled. "Be fine."

Carolyn picked up her radio and called in the two drunks. She wasn't used to so much direct contact with the students. Her shoulder hurt so she moved it around to keep it loose.

After the van came by and she called in her report, Carolyn headed back to the office. Her shift was done, her territory policed for tonight. In her street clothes now, she left the locker room.

Tucked among the water and waste buildings at the back of the campus, the security offices had little foot traffic late at night. Carolyn began her run, letting her legs warm up and feeling the muscles stretch. Dampness remained in the air from the rain during the day. Pools of water dotted the trail ahead. Her homeward path took her between various brick buildings as she found a comfortable pace across the campus.

The footpaths through the cemetery were dirt and woven with troughs where streams of water had dug into the ground, the trail was worn flat and hard by students who passed through to classes. Carolyn had traveled this way often and ran without hesitation. Her running suit added a swoosh sound as she ran, like a rhythm section keeping time to the beat.

She heard a click nearby. She thought it was just a sound in the night. A hand locked onto her wrist. A heavy boot thudded. There was sharp pain in her shoulder as she was jerked around. Instincts made her lash out with a free arm toward her hand. The flash and swipe of a blade made her pull away from the grip on her wrist. The blade caught the side of her face as she fell. The hand grasping her wrist held tight, she pushed up, ignored the pain, and leaped at her attacker. Carolyn hit him with her fist and he fell roughly to the ground. The grip on her wrist relaxed and she twisted away. She propelled herself up, away, and ran.

She hit the street and pushed hard, each step lifted her up and she flew along. Her own breathing and the sound of her sneakers hitting pavement filled her ears. On her doorstep, she took deep breaths. Fumbling with the keys, she cursed the lock that blocked her. Once inside she sat down and began sobbing.

She went to her roommate's bedroom door and knocked. The door was open, the room was dark. Light from the hall sliced into the room illuminating an empty bed. Carolyn knew Sharon was working tonight but she was not supposed to be late. Carolyn would tell her tomorrow.

She called the police and reported what happened. Eventually she was told that officers would arrive shortly. What else could she do? Something horrible could have happened. That's what it came to, what *could* have happened. She stood up and paced around the apartment. Finally, lights fanned across the room through the front window. Pushing aside the curtain, she saw the headlights of a police car. Carolyn met the policewoman at the door.

Officer Jane Ferrin unfolded her log book and took notes. After identifying Carolyn and getting a phone number, she listened to the report of the attack.

"You don't recall the face of the attacker?" Ferrin asked.

"It was a man. It was too quick, too dark. I remember the sound, and feeling the knife. I panicked."

"No face, too bad." Ferrin scribbled in her book.

"I don't understand how he held my wrist so tight." She rubbed her wrist and flexed her hand.

"What do I do now?" she asked. "I work security at the University, but we're taught to hand off victims to police."

Ferrin closed up her notebook.

"I'll go over the path you took home, your description of the route is good and we know the area. If anything comes up we'll get back to you. Do you have someone who can stay with you tonight?"

"My roommate is usually home by now. She must be working." She shook her head. "I don't have anyone else around."

"I'll get an extra patrol to drive through tonight. If you decide you want to talk to someone, call me and I'll find help." She pulled a card out of her pocket and handed it to Carolyn.

"Thanks."

"There's not a lot of information about your attacker to go on, if you think of anything else let me know or drop by the station, I'll add it to the report."

After the officer left, Carolyn made a call to Sharon De LaFleur's cell phone. The call connected and automatically went to voice mail. After ringing off, she wondered where Sharon could be. Normally she checked in. Finally, Carolyn felt strong enough to turn off the extra lights in the apartment. She settled in for the night. Another half an hour passed as she lay in bed imagining what could have happened.

Unable to sleep, Carolyn got up. Being alone tonight was not good, she thought. Gathering clothes into a gym bag, she wondered who to call so late at night. In her room, she showered and then changed into jeans and a heavy pullover.

Carolyn heard a scratching sound, then the tinkling of glass. A draft of air moved through the room. A door handle rattled. She laced her shoes and doused the light. All of the lights went out. She made her way to the front door. Carolyn ran out to the parking lot and jumped into her car. She stabbed her keys into the ignition and the car jumped to life. In the rear view mirror she saw the curtain move. When she looked back an angry face peered through the window.

Chapter Five

Reports from interviews were beginning to come in. Madison started at the top and opened a file from Officer Ferrin. A home invasion had taken place the same day that Sharon De LaFleur was found. It had been called in by Carolyn Pendle who lived at the same address as De LaFleur. Officer Ferrin said the apartment had been invaded at around two on Monday morning. The apartment had been entered through a window. Inside the apartment, drawers were opened, papers had been scattered around, but Carolyn couldn't tell if items were missing. At the officer's suggestion Carolyn was advised to find another place to stay for the evening. A contact phone number for Carolyn was left in the report. Madison tried the number but no one picked up. Madison decided to visit the Winsome Arms Apartments.

Close to the university, the apartment complex looked its age. The overall impression was that these units hadn't been maintained well over time. Madison pushed the button for the bell. He didn't hear a bell ring. No one appeared at the door after several rings and knocks. A man approached him across the lawn.

"You need something?" said the man.

"Detective John Madison, North Glendon police." He held out an ID card. "I'm looking into an incident from a few days ago. A break in."

"Barry Green, maintenance super." Green wore blue jeans and a tan work shirt. He was dirty, even his paint stained shoes were lined with mud. In his late thirties, his face was scruffy and he carried garden tools. He walked with a slight gait and stood favoring one leg. He had the beginnings of a belly that stretched his shirt and tested his buttons.

"Do you know about the women who lived here then?"

"Depends on what you need to know. I don't keep tabs on everyone, just make sure the place is neat and plumbing and electric are working."

"What about Carolyn Pendle and Sharon De LaFleur? Do you know them?"

"You mean, did I? Ms. De LaFleur is dead according to the papers and Ms. Pendle hasn't been seen for a few days. No, I didn't know either of them."

"You ever see them out and about? Could you identify them if you saw them?"

"Maybe Ms. De LaFleur. I might know her, I've seen her a few times going out, probably to work. Slacks and white shirt, but she always walked out, no car. She leaves in the late afternoon or evening." He leaned toward Madison, his breath tainted with beer and onions. "It's too bad about her. Seemed like a reliable sort of girl. I never had trouble with noise or damage of any sort. Not with her."

"What about Carolyn Pendle?"

"Don't recall seeing her much. Probably just kept to herself." He shifted and glanced away, he was done with this conversation.

Madison thought Barry Green was holding something back. He wasn't acting nervous like most people who talk with police. His responses seemed rehearsed, like he was expecting this conversation.

"Were they regular about rent, did they ever have money problems?"

"Not that I know, but I don't do anything with rent. I buy hardware and parts to fix plumbing and walls and windows, that's out of petty cash or store accounts we've got."

"Have you seen any unusual activity around here lately?"

Barry shifted from foot to foot before he answered.

"De LaFleur had a break in last night. Your people came by."

"Did you show up?"

"Nope. Just patched the window this morning when I got the call from the office."

"Ms. Pendle didn't call to get it fixed?"

"Nope. Take a look around by the kitchen door, I patched it right away."

"Show me." Madison followed Barry around the building to the back door. A piece of cardboard had been cut and taped to the glass in the door.

"It was busted in, glass on the kitchen floor. Someone was thrashing around the place. Furniture moved around, messy."

"Could I get a look inside?"

"Can I call my boss about the rules on that?"

"I can get a search warrant if you like." Madison pulled his out his cell phone.

Barry grunted then made his own call.

"It looks like you're going to get a look in. Office said they haven't been paid for this month, come on."

The back door was metal with the upper half a mullioned window of nine panes. Barry unlocked the door and they walked into the kitchen. The kitchen looked clean which seemed odd to Madison. The report said it was a mess. He noticed a shard of glass stuck under the baseboard along the wall. He shoved it around with his shoe until it released, then pulled a handkerchief out of his pocket, and picked up the shard. It was a clean sliver, sharp-edged and holding it to the light he thought he saw a fingerprint. He pulled an evidence bag from his pocket, labeled it and slid the glass inside. Perhaps the lab could get an ID.

Barry stared out the window, unconcerned about Madison's probing. "Look," he said, "When you're done here, just close the door. I'm gonna go get some work done."

"Did the place look like this when you came to fix the glass?" Madison asked.

"Sort of."

"Which means?"

"I shifted stuff a bit, kinda cleaned a little."

"You mean Carolyn Pendle wasn't here when you came over?"

"Nope. Not at seven this morning she wasn't."

"You do know she had an officer here and made a burglary report last night, right?"

"I didn't see anything. I was over this morning, cleaned up and left. It's not my business."

Madison saw a man, likely with a record, getting nervous.

"I'm going to look around, if I take anything out, I'll leave a receipt. I may need to talk with you again."

Barry left. Silence settled into the apartment, Madison moved from room to room touching little as he went, observing, and trying to get a picture in his mind of who Sharon De LaFleur was. The absence of photos suggested no close family. The mess was either the result of the break in or indicated a lack of interest in cleaning, probably the break in. The books he found were a mix of topics, murder mystery, romance, psychological studies/thrillers. He saw travel guides, cookbooks, two textbooks on literature and a few religious tomes. There was also a Bible, handbooks on solitude and techniques for relaxing. Madison wondered if De LaFleur had conflict or anger issues.

The silence was broken by his cell phones ring tone.

"Hi, Doc, what did you find?" 'Doc' was Doctor Jeanne Winslow, medical examiner for the North Glendon police department. "Oh, really?" he said. "Does that happen often?" He made notes in his notebook.

"That's not good. What do you do now?" He listened. "Thanks," he said. "I'll get on it."

He frowned to himself as he put away the phone and shoved his notes into his pocket. He'd get to the final report when he got back to the office. For now he wondered exactly how Sharon De LaFleur's heart had stopped. Dr. Winslow didn't know. The detective finished his tour of the apartment. Something didn't look right but he couldn't see what it was. It was time to get back to the office for another look at the De LaFleur crime scene evidence. And Madison wondered what had happened to Carolyn Pendle.

Chapter Six

One mile north of the Newsome Hotel, east of Main street, sat a run-down two story house with two dilapidated outbuildings. It was the sort of property avoided by passersby. Some hoped the city would condemn it. In the last few years the house had become decrepit, it had shrunken into itself as though it were infected or forbidden. Close to the house there was a dank smell, like weeds left rotting in dirt. Isolated, spurned by everyone, unwholesome, smelly; it was perfect.

On the far side of the property, the side which skirted the alley, there was a lightly tamped path that started in the corner under the briars and reached into the grasses heading toward the house. The trail led to the back of the house and then to one of the outbuildings. Trios of tall fir trees grew in huddles dotting the property. Pine cones were stippled across the upper branches of the firs. The trees were encased in blackberry vines that melted into the lower branches forming a green mottled ball of vine and tree.

On this Wednesday night a breeze startled an owl and a varmint whispered through the grass. Nothing outside the house indicated the presence inside. In the large central room by the front window, a dark green tarp, a plastic tipi, was held up by wooden and metal poles that were cobbled together. In the tipi a mattress covered by blankets lay on one side of the space. A table made from two fruit boxes sat in the middle. A cup and a short stack of plates were sitting together on top of the boxes. A candle smelling of roses burned in the corner and masked the other smells that permeated the room.

In another corner resting on concrete blocks was a camp stove. A woman was hunched over the stove. Dark liquid boiled in the pot before her, the woman's next meal. She mumbled to herself as she added dry noodles to the boiling liquid. The candle flickered as she breathed across it. The young lady wore loose fitting pants, athletic shoes, and a collared shirt under a dark cotton jacket. Her face strained as she glanced around the tent for something. "Poison," she muttered. With a practiced turn, she shed the dark outer garments of coat and jogging pants, then grabbed up a sweatshirt and jeans from the end table close by. These were clean and warm.

The heat from the boiling soup was adding to the warmth generated by a space heater purring near the mattress. The young woman reached into a bag that lay open on the floor. She pulled out several sticky mouse traps. She switched on her head lamp, opened the flap of the tarp and walked out. She placed the traps throughout the house. The minutes that passed while she spread the traps were enough to cook the noodles on the camp stove. She grabbed the pot and then sat on the mattress to eat and think.

How did it come to this? Why was she scrambling to survive when only a few days ago she was living her life comfortably? Who was trying to get to her anyway? And what had happened to her roommate?

As she had for the last few days, Carolyn Pendle ran these questions through her mind over and over. She had plenty of questions and few answers, odd threads from different fabrics, nothing that wove itself into whole cloth.

Carolyn sat down and tried not to remember that night. But the memories flared up again. Her eyes closed tight, the details not forgotten; it still didn't make sense to her. How did he find her apartment so fast? Who was he? Why did he keep going after her? Her escape seemed like ages ago, but it was only forty-eight hours. She had stolen out during the day to get cash and supplies, but paranoia was beginning to creep in to her mind. Was she really someone's target? Whatever happened to Sharon?

Calls to her friends at work didn't pan out. Officer Ferrin didn't respond to her call later that night and Carolyn didn't trust her anyway. As she ran through the possibilities for her immediate future, her imagination told her that someone must have found her ID in the apartment and was using it to locate her.

Panic had taken her to the empty house where she was now. This was the first home she had stayed in when she moved to North Glendon, when she started her college education. Empty after the newest owner died and the taxes came due, the house had been abandoned when the estate languished in the courts. She had returned and camped out. No one knew where she was. She would be safe here. In the past.

Outside the air began to chill as a breeze moved out of the valley and rose into the hills. A flurry of moisture hurled sideways then swooped down and died in the brown puddles that dotted the property. Carolyn hoped the chill was just in the weather and wasn't an indicator of worse events to come.

Light played through the narrow blinds above Jeffrey Grants' head. He opened his eyes. Three twelve in the morning. He heard breaking glass. In the dark, he went to the closet and pulled down the shoe box on the shelf. He pulled out an old Colt .38 and slid the clip out. At the nightstand he picked up three cartridges and slid them into the clip.

He walked down the hallway listening. Strips of light fell onto the floor in the living room. It was empty. He moved to the kitchen. It was quiet. Relieved, he stood in the kitchen and listened. He heard a trickle of water in the gutters, raining, he thought. Then he saw a flash of a light outside and heard glass breaking. In the living room he pulled the venetian blinds open at the edge, he could just see out. There was movement in the neighbor's yard. A motion sensor kicked on a light and a dark shape dropped into the bushes close to by. He stepped out the front door and slipped around the hedge to his neighbor's yard.

"What are you up to, young man?" A voice said. Jeffrey knew who it was right away.

"It's me, Jimmy," said Jeffrey. "Jeffrey Grant, next door."

"Grant? Did you hear it too?" Jimmy walked over, slippers swished through the grass and he was even more disheveled than Jeffrey. He wore a gray robe and low-slung undershirt, a flashlight probed the grass in front of him and he flipped the beam up into Jeffrey's face for a second. In his late sixties, Jimmy loped along with determination. Overweight by fifty pounds, he carried it all in his belly.

"I thought I saw someone in the brush by your house. I guess they're gone now," Jeffrey said.

"I came around from the back, no broken glass here, though I know I heard glass break."

"You didn't see anyone?"

"Nope, they might have heard me." He wiped the rain off of his face. "They're gone. And it's too wet to hang and talk."

"I wonder what they were looking for?"

"Not much here to steal that's for sure." Jimmy was a retired mill worker who kept his house and property neat.

"I don't think there's much of my stuff he'd want. Not even a nice car to steal." Jeffrey wiped his face of rain and nodded to Jimmy. "I'm going in, keep an eye out."

Jeffrey stopped at the front door before he went in. He surveyed the shadows around the yard and the pools of light along the street, the sound of steps on a rough surface drew near. He's still out there, he thought. It sounded like he was on the other side of the duplex, Mrs. Henson's side. Jeffrey had to take a look.

He went down the steps and around to the back and side yards. He moved quietly along the grass and felt himself tense up as he rounded the corner. He tightened his grip on the gun in his pocket. Hunched over he strained to see into the shadows along the side of the house. He felt the tension increase in his shoulders. Silence descended on the scene, his senses were on high alert. An eerie feeling of calm enveloped him as peered into the night. The open area seemed bright and Jeffrey needed a few seconds to let his eyes adjust to the change. He heard the squelch of a footstep on soggy earth and the distinct whip of a fast moving object. He felt an impact on his face then he blacked out and fell to the ground.

The chittering of a squirrel broke the silence. It was loud. He felt damp all around him. His face was being pelted with water, it was raining. He must not be in bed, he thought. The pain hit hard. He lifted his hand to wipe the water away which brought the pain to a higher pitch. After the sharp pain settled, he tried again. As he moved his shoulders leaves slipped off his chest. He saw a yellow light. Soaked to the skin, his head hurt, his eyes hurt, and his hand was now covered with a dark crusted substance.

He made an effort to get up and found he had fallen into a bush. Why was he here? Pushing himself up from the ground in spite of the pain he felt stiff, cold, and uncertain. His eye sight had partially returned. His face hurt. He wondered if the crusty substance was blood.

Jeffrey made his way back into the house and began cleaning up. It was past four in the morning. After a shower he bandaged his face as best he could. The pounding in his head was overwhelming. He swallowed two ibuprofens. He figured he must have fallen, slipped on something and hit his head. Could it have been that? He must have fallen pretty hard. He remembered walking around the front of the house. He had heard a noise before he turned the corner. Then he remembered blinding pain.

Chapter Seven

"What happened to you?" Madison said. Jeffery's right eye was blackened. A red lump spread from the skin by his ear up to the hairline and across half his forehead. Madison could tell these wounds were new. He would look bad and feel worse later.

Madison turned on the recording unit and the interview began. Again, Jeffrey described the attack in his yard.

"This is Detective John Madison, North Glendon Police Department, talking with Jeffrey Grant, interview room one. Please state your name."

"Jeffrey Grant."

"Would you like to have council present at this interview?"

"No, I'm fine for now."

"The last time we talked you seemed reluctant. Since then, I've received information from the California Department of Corrections, DJJ, Department of Juvenile Justice. They say you've been rehabilitated."

Jeffry sat back in the chair gaping. "That's expunged."

"Apparently not."

"I was a kid then."

"A girl died. Kathleen Richmond."

"I didn't do it."

"Are you talking about Richmond or De LaFleur?"

Jeffrey slammed his hands on the table and stood up.

"I didn't kill either of them. You're not listening."

Madison stood up. "Sit down. Tell me about Richmond. I'm listening."

"It was a party. There were six of us on a trip to the beach. After the bonfire I went for a walk on the dunes, Kathy walked away after I did. Everyone was drinking, getting high. When I came back she was still gone. Everyone crashed until morning. We all went looking for her and one of the others found her."

"Why did they think it was you?"

"We'd been making out on the drive over. We were just friends."

Madison slid a folder over to Jeffrey. "Take a look at the pictures."

Jeffrey slid the chair back and crossed his arms. "I've seen them."

"They found her necklace in your pocket. Her DNA was under your nails."

Jeffrey dropped his head to his chest.

"Let's talk about Sharon De LaFleur now. What did you take of hers?"

The interview was over. Two days after finding her and Jeffrey was at the top of the list again.

He pushed through the door of the station and felt the rush of air exchange with the outdoors. It was cool and fresh outside compared to the staleness inside the building.

He paused at the top step. The air felt cleansing, but he couldn't make the same claim about his own thoughts. Why didn't he believe it right away? They would naturally suspect him first, he found the body. That was how they showed it on television. They got to his juvenile record without a hitch. The pain in his head was stronger. He wanted to run but didn't know where to go.

At home, Jeffrey called Bill Clemons.

"You have time to talk?" He heard muted conversation in the background then Bill came back.

"So what's going on?" said Bill.

"Two things. Someone attacked me last night and the police had me in for another interview."

"Who attacked you? When?"

Jeffrey told him the story about the attack.

"You gonna be okay?"

"Yeah. A black eye, scrapes around my face and maybe a concussion, but that's it."

"How about your hands?"

"I can still play guitar. No permanent damage."

"You think it's related to Sharon?"

"I don't know. If it is, how did they know about me? Or even where I live?"

"True. It could be random."

"And I just got out of an interview with the detective again. They called me in this morning."

"You thought they might. Is that bad?"

"They know about California."

"Ah."

"I've got to be their prime suspect." Jeffrey's voice had pitched up a little.

"Not necessarily. What sort of questions did they ask? *'Where were you on the night of...'*

"No, more details on my walk home that night. I'm wondering if I should be talking to a lawyer."

"Do you know any lawyers?"

"Not on purpose."

"Could be time."

"That's what I'm afraid of."

"What would you do?"

"You know I'm cautious. I'd get someone right away. Since my experience at Berkeley I don't trust officials much."

"Maybe I will."

"It couldn't hurt to find out. All you've got to lose is money."

"Thanks. I'm thinking. It might be worth it."

"Jeffrey, I hate to cut you off, but I've got to get my next lesson started. I'll talk to you later."

Jeffrey hung up and did a search on criminal lawyers. The list of names he found was way too long for a town the size of North Glendon. He sent the names to the printer. How had he gotten to this point? Why was he the one to find Sharon? What should he be doing now? This lawyer search didn't feel right to him.

He paced the room as he debated in his mind. Worried and worn out, time caught up with him as he went through scenarios for his future. None of them looked good. Jeffrey passed out in his recliner. He slept fitfully.

Jeffrey woke realizing what he had to do next. He needed to figure out what happened on his own since they weren't doing it. He called one of the lawyers on his list and arranged to be represented. Next, he needed to start asking questions.

Bill Clemons watched Jason Williams. Jason fitted the drumstick awkwardly into his hand.

"Okay, you've got the sticks, now the next step is to make them bounce on the drum head, not to pound it."

"But I want to make noise," said Jason. He beat the drum wildly.

"And you will, but let's make it music too." Bill picked up his sticks and mirrored Jason. "Look here. Play this pattern first."

After the lesson, he wondered what was up with Jeffrey. Then he wondered about himself. He'd been out with Sharon but they soon agreed it wouldn't work out. Their argument had been loud and heard by everyone.

"Get your hands off me," Sharon said. She backed away.

"It's a good night hug," Bill said.

"It's good night with no hug," she said.

The Jazz Room was silent and everyone had turned to them when their voices got loud.

"What's wrong with you anyway?"

"Nothing a perv like you needs to know."

"What?" Bill took a step toward De LaFleur.

"Get away. I'm leaving." She turned and ran away.

Bill stood shaking his head.

Jeffrey walked into the Jazz Room. Light from the doorway made his shadow stretch out into the darkness of the room. The exit lights spaced around the room punctuated the darkness. Jeffrey walked into the equipment room that held the employee lockers. He pulled out a guitar case, found his list of hotel employees and left the room.

Jeffrey went to the employees break room. On the far wall were three neat rows of matching lockers. Padlocks hung from some of the doors. Jeffrey looked for Sharon De LaFleur's locker number from the employee list. He tried to get a look into the locker, but the metal fins weren't angled so he could see inside.

At the front desk, Jeffrey logged into the computer and checked out the work schedule. Along with Jimmy Barlow working the bar, the list included Gina Posey, Bonnie Cho and Sharon De LaFleur working the tables.

De LaFleur was scheduled for Thursday through Sunday evenings. She had also worked Sunday night half a shift. She would have closed out the room every night.

"What are you doing, Jeff?" Gina Posey walked up to the desk. She looked cheerful in a patterned blouse and slacks.

"What are you doing here so early?" he asked, startled.

She slipped a large bag off her shoulder and put it on the counter.

"Shopping nearby and it's too heavy to carry around. Gonna work tonight so I thought I'd drop it off." She smiled a little too wide. Gina was happy to a fault and it usually bothered her co-workers to no end.

"Usually you don't show until the last minute."

"Just checking out the schedule," he said.

"But you already know what nights you guys play," she said.

"It's not for me, I'm checking out other schedules."

"So who's your new interest? Maybe you're looking up my schedule so you can bump into me after work?"

Jeffrey winced. While Gina was a pretty woman at twenty eight, she was also known to regularly date and drop men on a whim.

Jeff said, "I'm checking something out, but not you."

Gina stared at him.

"I'm trying to find out about Sharon De LaFleur," he said. "Looking to see what her schedule would have been. Maybe it'll tell me something."

"What do you mean would have been? Did she quit? She didn't say anything to me. You'd think if she was leaving she'd let me know. Kind of a courtesy, you know?"

"You don't know?"

"Don't know what?"

"How could you know, it probably didn't make the news. They just identified her."

"What happened? What do you mean identified her? What are you talking about?"

"Sharon is dead. Sunday night."

Gina dropped into a chair.

"Dead," she said. "What happened?"

"I'm not sure," Jeffery replied. "Things have been blurry since then."

Jeffrey told her about his discovery of the body, not knowing who it was, then about being interviewed by the police and then learning that it was Sharon.

"What do you think happened, Jeff?"

"I don't know. I talked to her Sunday during the last break."

"She's dead. It just doesn't make sense."

Others joined them. Two of the housekeepers coming on shift, Teresa and Oliver, both newcomers to the area and still getting used to the winter rains. Connie Flagston, bookkeeper and assistant manager, had arrived.

"So who's the gossip about?" said Connie.

"Sharon De LaFleur." Gina said.

"What now?"

"She died Sunday night. Jeffery found her on the way home."

"Our Sharon? What do you mean? Who would do that?" Connie threw her arms out as she spoke. "There was an article in the paper. That was Sharon?"

"Nobody knows what happened," said Jeffrey. "I was questioned by the police. They think I may have something to do with it. I don't. I just found her."

"What do you mean found her?" said Connie.

"I mean walking home Sunday night, I found her. She was lying under a hedge near the university. I didn't even know it was her until the detective told me."

"Don't you remember people's faces? You've talked with her," said Connie.

"Of course I do, but late at night, it was dark, facing away, I couldn't tell who it was. I've never come across this sort of thing before. I don't think you'd do any better if you'd have found her."

"All right. It just seems strange not to know who it is no matter what the situation."

Steven Grange walked up. Steven was the security department for the Newsome. He was also the only full-time security member.

"So you made the discovery, eh?" said Steven.

"How did you find out?" asked Jeffery.

"I read the papers for a start. But my real source is in the department. You've got some explaining to do, buddy. Not everyone thinks you're clean for it."

"Clean for what?"

"Her death, of course. If you didn't work here, you might have gotten away with it."

Jeffrey took control of himself.

"I don't like what you're suggesting."

"Sure," said Steve.

Jeffrey picked up the papers and got up to go. Gina reached over and grabbed his arm.

"He's just pushing your buttons, Jeff." Gina said. "Ignore him. Let it ride. Sharon never let anyone close to her that I know of. Why would you be singled out anyway? Nobody really knew her."

Chapter Eight

D eBrough walked into Madison's office.

"I had interesting interviews at the Newsome last night. Looks like Sharon De LaFleur dated two of the musicians. Neither one for long, and one ended with an argument." DeBrough slid a folder with the interviews across the desk.

"Was it Jeffrey Grant?"

"No, Clemons. William Clemons. Lots of people saw the argument."

"Was it violent?"

"No. It was loud. Clemons acted aggressive according to one of the servers."

"So let's check out Clemons. See if he's got a history."

"I still like Grant for it. We dig deep enough and the evidence will show up."

"It looks like Grant to me. But check out Clemons anyway."

Madison wondered about this turn of events. Very little real evidence pointing to Jeffrey Grant and now he had another actor to check on. He also needed to know more about Sharon De LaFleur.

Eddie grasped the door handle and jerked hard. Lately the lock had been catching on the back door of the cargo van. After his delivery he could go to the warehouse to pick up the next shipment he had placed for meds. His enterprise was moving along smoothly now. The income wasn't as much as he had hoped but five thousand every other week would get him out of town sooner than later. He hated the rain that permeated the valley. It neither poured nor misted properly, it was like a shower head that was obstructed. The clouds leaked water, then they sprayed fist fulls of moisture that would worm its way into your garments and get you soaked to the skin. Eddie always felt damp. He hated it.

Today the prospect of liberating himself from the mistake that the waitress at the Newsome had made would finally be over. He felt in his bones that he was close to getting that paperwork back. The police would call it evidence, the invoice for the meds could be tracked back to him. He off-loaded the boxes into the storage room at the hotel.

"Who wants to sign for this stuff," he asked.

"Better get Mr. Florence to check it out. He's up front," said a custodian.

"Thanks." The double doors into the lobby opened automatically and he walked out to the front desk.

"Mr. Florence?" said Eddie. The man was signing papers and answered without looking up.

"Yes?"

"Cleaning supplies, can I get a signature for receipt? I left the boxes in the storage room as usual."

"And you are?"

"Highway Cargo. I brought cleaning stuff this time. My name's Eddie."

"Let's see the invoice."

Eddie scooted the papers to him.

"Not electronic yet?" asked Mr. Florence.

"Not yet."

He signed the papers, gave them back to Eddie and went back to work. Back at the van, Eddie mimicked the man, "Not electronic yet? Jerk." He slammed the van into gear and left.

The flashlight's beam scanned the ceiling of the room. The light moved left to right, then down to reveal a stack of boxes. A dry, papery smell permeated the room. The boxes were stacked high and four deep against the walls. Eddie saw new cobwebs had appeared since his last visit. He'd have to clean these out on his next trip. The light startled a house spider. It scuttled back into the corner.

He sat the flashlight on a box. It gave off enough light to allow him to work. He shifted a few boxes to the side. The change revealed a narrow path that went to the back of the storage room. He scooted sideways down the path. The flashlight illuminated his sneakers as he moved along the boxes. When he reached the back, there was a small cove, a cavern in the corner.

He opened a box and pulled out a small shoe box. He was alone. Eddie felt a calmness fall upon him. He reached into his pocket and pulled out the trinkets to add to his collection. The earrings, shiny copper plate with black stones, were warm in his palm. He felt good right now, close to peace. He dumped the earrings into the box. With the addition of the earrings the bottom of the box didn't look so empty. So many small bits and pieces and such a big box to fill, he thought. Eddie exhaled. His mind cleared.

He wanted to procure more baubles. Eddie took his finger and scooted some of the earrings, rings, and necklaces around. Each brought back a memory. Sometimes he only stole the rings. Sometimes he had to hurt someone. This was the first time he had taken a life. He liked it.

He was having a harder time remembering the details about the older items. That was happening more often these days. He closed the lid and placed the box inside the carton. He reversed himself out of the corner, shuffling quietly. The space seemed to have gotten tighter. Perhaps he had gained weight. He didn't like the thought of extra baggage. He'd always kept reasonably trim. To him excess fat reflected laziness. Eddie wouldn't tolerate that. At thirty-five it was time for him to exercise more.

He took one last look around. His flashlight revealed a simple storage bin. It contained lots of boxes with pharmaceutical labels on them. He closed the door and locked the storage locker. He pulled out an orange plastic tag, looped the tail through the clasp and secured it to the lock. Eddie wrote his initials on the tag, then added an eight digit series of numbers that matched the paper he held in his wallet. The orange tag would have to be cut to open the storage room door. It was his secondary security system.

As he walked along the corridor, fluorescent lights crackled above him. It looked like something out of an old movie. He thought movies were so stupid. They always wore those black oxfords. The leather soles were way too slick to run in, and you couldn't keep quiet no matter what.

His mind raced back to last night. Had he really cleaned up his mistake? Was getting rid of the girl enough? As he neared the exit he tugged down his baseball cap and pushed his sunglasses up the bridge of his nose. Eddie walked to the door, punched in his access code and left.

The white cargo van Eddie drove sported no emblems, the wheels and tires were standard issue, black and nameless. Confident in his anonymity, he drove away from the storage facility and into the evening. He watched a swallow flip by his window as he drove on down the road. Did that mean something? A portent maybe?

Eddie considered scenarios for the days to come. Like a musician struggling to learn a new song. Eddie played scenes over and over in his mind until they felt right. He crossed poison off his mental checklist of ways to kill a person. The girl's death the other night hadn't been as interesting as he had hoped. It didn't take much to get the liquid into her drink nor was it difficult to figure out the dosage that would kill her. He was disappointed that she had dropped earlier than he wanted. And that guy had found her too soon but he would get him back for interfering. Eddie remembered the way the scene had played out.

Staying in the shadows, he followed the waitress when she left the hotel. She was easy to follow. What was disconcerting to Eddie was that the poison kicked in before she got to her apartment. She made quick steps through the cemetery as before. Scuffling the twigs and dirt, she walked down the path that took her near the headstones and statuary. She startled at a bat that flew out of a tree. She was near the end of the path and ready to walk down to the street when she stopped. He saw her raise her hands to her ears. She lost her balance, then she grabbed the railing. Her head tilted, she covered her ears again and walked drunkenly along the sidewalk.

Sharon felt a thick fog envelope her head. It cleared for a moment. She knew she had walked through the cemetery, but couldn't remember how long ago that was. She stepped ahead, seeking out the hedge that told her she was close to her apartment. Then it felt as though the light was closing down. Darker, muddier, she seemed to be moving but in a dream. She was being watched. A wandering eye, dark blue and black crossed her vision. She knew it wasn't real, maybe. She grabbed something. She looked at it and then blacked out.

Eddie watched as she fell. He thought that he must have been off on her weight. The liquid should have dropped her when she got home. Oh, right, he remembered. The effects are gradual they slowed her down then came the disorientation. Have to remember that, he thought. He moved closer, her breathing sounded labored. She was taking a while to expire. He'd have to follow close now.

He wouldn't leave footprints, he thought. He leaned over the railing and saw her on the ground behind the hedge. She laid face down, flat on the ground. He could see her back move with her gasping breaths. There was silence, then a hurried intake of air. Her last exhale was mostly silent, he saw her back relax, and then she stopped breathing.

Eddie clicked on the headlamp he pulled from his pocket. He slipped on latex gloves. He knelt down by her on the grass. He watched her and began to float away in his mind. He imagined touching her starting with the top of her head. He leaned in and smelled the shampoo from her hair. He pressed and kneaded the skin around her ears then moved to her face and touched her eye lids, the bridge of her nose, caressed her upper lip sensually. In his mind he quietly, effortlessly, methodically, worked his way down until he reached the soles of her feet. Every bit of clothing was buttoned, moved, and replaced. His imagination reveled. When he was done he had memorized his victim. He knew her now unlike any other he had known. He let out an inaudible sigh; his time with the lovely lady was at an end.

On reflection, Eddie was pleased with the results. He'd never used poison before and was surprised at how accurate his research had been. She died about thirty minutes after taking the poison; he would have to note the gradual onset of the effects. When he administered it, she hadn't even noticed. Eddie had expected trouble. He inserted a hand into her pocketbook and rifled through the contents. Nothing ominous or threatening was available. He decided to take the whole thing and filter through it later. He removed her earrings and stuffed them in his pocket.

Chapter Ten

It was evening and Carolyn walked with purpose. She felt the damp chill of autumn sinking into her bones. The breeze on her cheeks moved along her neck and down her back like the unwanted touch of a stranger. She glanced around and tugged the zipper on her jacket a little higher. Her shoes on the pavement sounded musical, like a wet percussion section swishing to a soggy beat. Silhouettes of oak trees loomed over the sidewalk ahead. It would be the perfect place for someone to hide, perfect for someone to leap out, stab her, and then disappear in the night.

Beyond the oak trees Carolyn could see a van sitting in a driveway. There was enough space beside it to keep someone hidden. No cars, no lights, no people walking at night, no animals roused from their hunting routines. She felt a rising tension. Didn't the birds talk among themselves when a stranger drew near? She felt a knot forming in the space between her shoulders. A lonely tune sung by Dan Fogelberg came back to her. Words about being on the road and long nights alone and wondering when he'd be home again. She didn't get the tune right and made up her own words. It was better than the silence for now. Now the tune was stuck in her head.

She didn't know if the papers she found at the apartment were important, but they could be. The only way to know was to figure out what they were for. She could go to the police, but knew they wouldn't believe her. That was true especially when they found out about her past. She'd been told it always comes back to haunt you.

Knowledge is supposed to be power, but for Carolyn the knowledge of what her mother had done to her father drained her day by day. The years of haranguing and fights that broke most of their dishes, the fear that her or her brother would be caught in the battle, countless nights of trying to cover up the sound of their violence by hiding under blankets and pillows weighed heaver on her.

She remembered her father as a quiet man; he worked at a dirty job. He came home hoping for rest, too tired to fight. Then in her thirteenth year, he died. No one talked about it to her. Her mother withdrew afterward and began her own decline into death. Her brother graduated from high school that same year and supported the family with part time jobs. She and Dan became the family when her mother receded into her room. Dan ran the household and became Carolyn's mentor, mother, and father. She copied the strength she saw in Dan and became a whole person over the next few years. Early in her last year of high school her mother died. Carolyn didn't remember any feelings about her mother's death. In some way it was a relief. She knew Dan would take care of her. She knew she could get along without her mother.

In her first year of university, Dan fell ill. In three months he became an invalid. The cancer moved quickly and was deadly. After graduation Carolyn sought out a roommate and met Sharon De LaFleur. Equally independent, Sharon kept to herself. They were both responsible enough to keep the place clean, and neither felt the need to become buddies even though they shared a living space.

And now here she was creeping back to her apartment to see if the paper she had found was key to Sharon's death. She kept herself on high alert as she neared the complex. Her plan was simple, get back into the apartment and find the book with the papers in them.

Detective Madison arrived at the station just after six o'clock, the sun was setting. Above the silhouetted trees an orange red sky slowly waned. Another day gone, thought John. What have I got to show for it? He sat in the car and thought about what he knew concerning the odd death of Sharon De LaFleur. She died late at night and seemed to be alone. Found by a musician who worked at the same hotel where Sharon worked. According to the ME there was no reason for her to be dead, other than her heart stopping. Tox reports were not back from the lab yet. She apparently had few friends but shared her apartment with a roommate.

Madison wondered if her roommate, Carolyn Pendle, knew something. And why would the apartment have been broken into? Was that related to the murder of Sharon or was that a coincidence? He didn't think it was coincidence. Was Pendle the target? At the front desk he stopped and spoke with Sergeant Bill Christy.

"Bill, when's Redman due back?" he asked.

Bill made a few clicks on the mouse and keyboard. He scanned through a screen with his finger.

"She's got another six days, John. What's up?"

"There's too much for one man to do. Six days." He shook his head. Madison's cell phone rang.

"I'm headed to my office, then over to you. Okay, thanks." He hung up the phone.

At this hour, the rest of the cubicles were empty. No catastrophes had come up in the last twenty-four hours so the other teams were taking advantage and bugging out as soon as possible. Madison decided to call his wife with the news of another late night. It rang through to the machine and he left a message.

"Looks like another late one, but I should be home before nine tonight. I'll call you before I leave. Bye." The ME report detailed what Dr. Winslow summarized by phone. Sharon De LaFleur died of heart failure. The ME's office was awaiting the results of toxicology tests. There were no indications of an external trauma; the liver mortis was not abnormal. Indications were that the victim had died and had not been moved from that place. No abrasions or unexpected bruising was noted. Her general health was good for a person of her age. There was no indication of intercourse in the twenty-four hours prior to her death. Nothing could reasonably be concluded about the death of Sharon De LeFleur other than the fact that she was dead and her heart had failed.

Going over the photographs, Madison noticed several indents in the grass that suggested someone had been there on their knees or crouching down. The positioning suggested access or contact with De LaFleur. It could have been the man who found the victim, or it could have been someone else.

At the Winsome Arms Apartments, Barry Green shifted from one cheek to the other. Wooden chairs caused S.B.S., sore butt syndrome. That one's funny, he thought. He lifted the binoculars again and resumed scanning the windows with lights. From his attic perch above the second floor apartment, Barry could see both entrances to the apartment complex. As the maintenance man, Barry felt it a privilege to have his pick of apartments. This one let him see the nocturnal goings on of the complex without being seen himself. He gained access to the attic and set up a viewing stand. For a man who liked to watch this was just right.

Barry would sit in the attic with a six pack of beer and watch the windows into the night. Tonight he checked out the windows in a pattern. In apartment eleven, second floor, no light in the main room, but light in the front bedroom. Yes. He squeezed the glasses to his eyes and refocused on the window. Her bedroom was next to the main room and the lamp by the bed cast a glow into the room. Her silhouette walked from the doorway to the bedside. Mrs. Drew had just returned from a run and was going to the shower, too bad she was in her fifties. He couldn't see skin so he moved on. A few windows over Barry saw a light flicker. He refocused the binoculars until the image sharpened. A flash of flesh. Female. He centered on the window and waited. It must be the daughter of Ms. Oakley, first name unknown. Those college kids were getting better and more exciting every year.

Carolyn kept to the darkest part of the sidewalk and slowed down. Down the block and across the street was the apartment complex. She expected little activity at one in the morning. At the corner she stopped and took a look around the maple tree that marked the corner of a yard. Across the street was her apartment. The sound of a pickup truck reached her. She stepped into the shadow of the tree. The sound of a squeal ripped the air. The darkness was pierced by headlights that crawled up to the stop sign. Carolyn slid further back into the darkness. More squeaks and squeals as it stopped, then the driver hit the gas pedal hard.

She waited. It was time to move. She followed a row of low bushes that skirted the edge of the property. Out of the corner of her eye, she noticed a flash of light above the apartment building next to hers. She stopped and dropped. No more light, no reflections. She made her way closer then dropped to her knees and listened. Carolyn heard the sound of crickets, a car moved along the road and died out. She knew where to look because she'd seen him before. She thought it was the maintenance man, Barry. She'd never had to talk to him, Sharon handled that, but he seemed a little sneaky, even slimy. The flash happened again. The maintenance guy was distracted. She used the moment to get to her apartment.

Once inside the apartment she could look out through the blinds. Nothing moved no one was around. The apartment smelled stale. She'd only been gone a few days. Carolyn stumbled through the apartment. The place was still a mess and hard to navigate. She pulled out the flashlight she brought with her and hoped it wasn't too bright. She didn't want any extra attention. The papers she had seen were in Sharon's books.

In the living room the books were stacked on three shelf units of different heights and indifferent construction. She replayed the scene of Sharon hiding the paper in her mind. She remembered standing in the doorway and Sharon picked up a heavy book with a black cover and slipped papers into it. Sharon had been startled when Carolyn entered the room and greeted her. She ran the light along the top left row and picked a book she thought was the right size. It was geometry, heavy and filled with diagrams on shiny paper. It contained no extra papers. Next she found a book on statistics. Lots of numbers, yet nothing added up. As she shook the book nothing fell out. Next, *The Complete Works of Shakespeare*. The book was thick as a brick and heavy. There were several sheets that fell out. Among them was an order form. The front scrap was a shipping label to a location in North Glendon from Juarez, Mexico. Attached to the shipping label was a supplier name and a list of the contents shipped. It noted receipt of eight boxes of eight bottles each. The chemical was labeled HCN and dated three weeks earlier. This one contained a signature that was hard to read. The first name was just a wavy line with a squiggle. The last name Carolyn took to be Smith or Smathe.

Chapter Eleven

T he last notes of "On Broadway" died out in a mix of muffled applause for Jeffrey Grant, Bill Clemons, and Harmon Webb. It was time for a break before the last set of the evening.

"What are you guys drinking?" asks Webb.

"Tonic water, ice and lime," said Jeffrey. "I'm going to get a breath of air, be back in a minute."

"You okay, Jeffrey?"

"Fine."

Not a bad crowd for a Thursday night, thought Webb. A mix of college kids, after dinner couples, and a few business travelers. He nodded at Teresa as she schlepped a tray of drinks. She smiled.

Harmon navigated through the tables. At the bar he gave a nod to Bonnie Cho as she picked up a tray of drinks and headed into the crowd. She looked as good as ever, he thought, even her slacks fit her smartly in the right places.

"Hey, Jimmy," he said. Perpetually happy, Jim Barlow worked silently. He filled orders put them onto a tray and nodded to Gina. She picked up the tray and was gone among the tables.

"What do you need tonight, Harmon?" asked Barlow.

"Two tonics with ice, one with lime, and a pint of Guinness."

"Got it," Barlow answered. "Sounds good tonight. Glad you guys keep bringing the crowds in."

"I'm shocked it's busy," said Harmon. "I thought people would be warming themselves by the glow of the electric blue tube."

Jim worked and talked. He topped off the beer and slid it to meet with the tonics.

"I'd say it's all the publicity about Sharon. In the paper they mentioned she worked here several times. Odd what brings people to a place." His hands were busy polishing glasses as he talked. "She seemed like a good girl, distracted the last few weeks though. She messed up lots of orders when she was on."

Harmon knew what was coming up and backed off the bar stool a little. He didn't know Barlow well and didn't want to talk about what he knew.

"You and her spent a little time together, didn't you?" said Barlow.

"Look, we went out a few times. She was nice, but we just didn't click." he picked up the drinks and left.

"I just shouldn't even try," muttered Harmon as he set the drinks down.

"I can't believe Sharon's gone," Clemons said. "I don't think I've ever known anyone who got killed."

Harmon ignored him.

"Whatever," Clemons said.

"A guitar player and a drummer were walking through a park one day. The guitar player said, 'Hey look at that dog with one eye!' The drummer covers one eye and says, 'Where?'"

Harmon didn't stir.

"Are you guys about ready?" said Jeffrey Grant. He grabbed his drink and set it on the amplifier.

He ran some scales to loosen up his fingers.

"Let's start off with number sixty-three then go right into sixty-four, Okay?"

He counted off the tempo for Thelonious Monks' "Straight No Chaser." The tune wound down smoothly. Clemons punched out the last chord with a downbeat and it was over.

Jeffrey began the chords to Cole Porter's "Love For Sale." There was a jarring clatter as the drums lost the beat and metal clanked on metal. Tilting forward Clemons was in pain, clenching himself into a fetal position. He lost control of his brushes. They clattered to the floor, he bent over to grab them and found himself unable to stop his momentum. A look of pain scrunched up his face. The music stopped. Bill Clemons fell onto the drums and cymbals, then everything under him seemed to collapse in slow motion. His face had a frozen expression of pain, then it relaxed. A breath of air left his mouth. Jeffrey dropped his guitar and vaulted to him.

"Bill," Jeffrey said. He pushed the drum out of the way and laid Clemons out flat. He pushed on his chest and began CPR.

"Call nine one one," he said. "Harmon, call now."

Chapter Twelve

T he glow of the LED display said it was two oh eight am. Detective John Madison slept soundly until his phone rang.

"Yeah, what's up?" he said, as he rubbed his eyes. "Right. And what makes you think it's related? The hotel. I'm up." He got out of bed and started dressing.

"Honey, I've got to work," he said. Then he remembered. Helen was gone and he was talking to himself again. When she had passed away three years ago, he had become withdrawn. He had always imagined himself dying first. Helen was supposed to live off his pension, go to the flower shows, spend time with her sisters and their families. He had always assumed she would be in the house after he was gone. After thirty-two years of marriage and without kids, the news of her cancer and the speed that it had taken over her body was overwhelming. In three months she was gone, in three months they had talked through more painful moments than in all the rest of their time together.

She was gone. He spent two months in solitude. He slept and read and watched the stars at night. He remembered their time. He cried and talked with her. He stared blankly at walls, heard her voice ring in his ears from the early years until their last conversations. He waited and listened to the house. He listened to the sounds of nature outside his doors. And he felt the burden of solitude in his soul.

Then one day, he opened the front door and went for a run. He spent a week rolling out of bed by noon and then reading. Counseling at the department helped. He missed his wife, but knew each day demanded his attention in a different way. On nights like tonight, being called out to a crime scene because it might be related to Sharon De LaFleur's murder was another day.

The lights inside the Jazz Room were up all the way but the room was still dark. Most of the customers had given statements to the officers and been released. A crime scene tech finished up the search he had been conducting on the stage area. The disarray of guitar, drums, keyboard, wires and music detritus provided a challenge for collecting evidence and finding prints that might be relevant. An officer with a feathered brush found and taped up fingerprints on the cymbals. She added another piece of tape to the sheet of prints, marked its location and made a few notes on the sheet. Trash from the EMS crew lay on the floor in front of the stage. Various kit bags were being packed up. Detective Madison noted as he walked in that this was the brightest he'd ever seen the place. He knew the hotel because this was where he and Helen came to dine and listen to the music.

"Madison," said detective Ron Marlin. They began going over the scene. He knew Sharon had worked here and he had already talked with the staff and read the interviews. Marlin told him about getting the call from responding officers for an ambulance and a VCU officer. The Violent Crimes Unit had three detectives for night calls and six for the day and evening shift.

"Looks like you're right," said Madison. "The same people are involved." He nodded over to Jeffrey Grant. Grant was slumped over in a chair by the stage.

"I don't want to interview Jeffrey Grant just now. Get one of the officers to go over what happened and I'll get to the band and staff after I see officers reports tomorrow." He gestured to the stage. "What does it look like so far?"

"It looks like the man collapsed. It might have been a heart attack. Nobody said they saw it begin. When the music stopped everyone noticed." Marlin pointed to the stage. "Grant was sitting to the right with his guitar, on the left was the piano player, Harmon Webb. They were playing and Grant and Webb just finished solos. The vic, William Clemons, the drummer, had just started his solo when he fell down. His fall knocked down drums and stands, but it doesn't look like he struggled. Grant and Webb both responded quickly and didn't hear Clemons speak or call out. Grant started CPR and Webb made the call to 9-1-1."

Marlin went looked at his notes. "Officers Arkin and Carpenter were close by and arrived in minutes. They reported that EMS was called right away and the area cordoned off. Carpenter took over CPR. Arkin made the call to dispatch for the ambulance. EMS crews arrived in eight minutes and they took over. They thought Clemons was dead already, but continued working on him until he was pronounced at the hospital."

"Sounds like a heart attack, but this guy doesn't seem old enough," said Madison. "They got any coffee over there? I need a pick up."

"Check it out. I think the barman's been interviewed already."

Jim Barlow poured two coffees and kept one for himself.

"How soon can I get out of here?" he said.

"That's up to Detective Marlin."

"Looks like you guys'll be here for a while."

"You know Clemons well?"

"No, said 'hi' when they got drinks, but he was only around for the gig, didn't hang with anyone else."

He didn't know what to think at this point, so he would wait. He wanted to fix the scene in his mind. There was a connection to the murder of De LaFleur, he just had to find it.

He walked around careful not to interfere with the techs. The main area seemed to be the stage. Clemons had fallen through a bunch of metal stands. One of the officers was interviewing Jeffrey Grant. Madison walked to a table within hearing range and sat down.

According to Grant, Bill Clemons just stopped moving and collapsed. Grant didn't see signs of life when they got to him. It was as though death had wrapped him up and smothered him, no resistance, no struggle, not a breath. To the left of the stage was a table with two glasses on it. One was an empty beer glass, the other a highball glass, tall and narrow. Madison motioned to a tech to make sure those items came back to the station.

On the stage was another glass, this one with clear liquid in it. There were also lots of cords, instruments and stands. The drums where Clemons sat were tipped in disarray.

"Did you guys tape your performances?" asked Madison.

"What?" Webb asked. "Tape them? We haven't used tape for years."

"No," said Jeffrey. "We've been playing so long most of the music is second nature. When we started we'd record it, not anymore."

"Did Clemons know Sharon De LaFleur well?" he asked.

"They dated a while back," said Jeffrey.

"Why did they break up?"

"I don't know. Bill didn't say."

"What do you think?"

"They were amicable. They seemed friendly."

It was an answer, but an incomplete answer, thought Madison.

"Was there any recent connection between them?"

"I didn't see anything new," said Jeffrey. Webb looked petulant.

"Are you saying they did or didn't have a relationship recently?"

"I'm saying I don't think so. Clemons didn't tell me everything about his personal life. Most of what I knew was from small talk on the breaks."

"So you didn't talk at other times?"

"No."

"Would your cell phone records reflect that?"

"Okay, calm down." Jeffrey said. "I talked to him yesterday at breakfast. We would meet about once a week."

Webb scowled at Jeffrey. "Why wasn't I invited?"

"It wasn't a combo meeting. It was coffee and conversation."

"How long were you doing this?"

"We began meeting a few months back. Clemons was going through some people problems. He would talk and I would listen."

"Did he have issues with De LaFleur?" asked Madison.

"I told you no." said Jeffrey. He sat back and crossed his arms.

Why was Grant being elusive? Perhaps the connection wasn't here and now, maybe it was something in the past. He'd have to check that out.

Both Jeffrey and Webb were sitting back in their seats with their arms crossed. It looked like the meeting was over.

As he walked out he realized that most anything could have happened. There were too many possibilities, not enough concrete evidence.

On his way out, he talked with Ron Marlin and voiced his immediate concerns. He nodded good byes to the crime scene crew and went to the office. Maybe the final autopsy report on De LaFleur would be ready.

His eyes hurt. Lack of sleep was always a problem with policemen and especially anyone called out for events like this. The possibility of making the front page of the Glendon Guardian didn't elude Madison. He knew reporters were already on the case and he'd be getting pressure from upstairs to solve this quickly. While a killer may have time to plan, he had to follow behind and make deductions from the evidence he found. He also had procedure and rules to follow. This case was not stacking up in Madison's favor.

Grant and Webb finished their interviews with the police. Within the hour the crime scene investigators had packed up and left. Clemons death hadn't sunk in yet, the busyness had kept them both distracted. Silence fell upon the room.

Packing up, Jeffrey and Harmon moved mechanically. Jeffrey walked around the drum kit and righted a cymbal stand and reset the snare drum. In his mind he would take a look back and see a flurry of hands and hear Bill pounding out rhythms that lifted the music to another level. That was something he'd miss about Bill Clemons. How could he be gone? The three of them complimented each other. Together they created music better than they could individually.

Now what would happen, he wondered. How would Harmon and he figure out what to do next? Did he need to find out who Bill was related to and tell them he was gone? What about taking care of Bill's stuff, who would do that?

Webb came over.

"Let's get out of here. We're tired."

"What about Bill?"

"We can't help him now."

"What do we do?"

"Rest, then figure it out tomorrow."

"What about Bill's family?"

"Tomorrow. I'm leaving."

Jeffrey watched as he walked away. He felt tired and old.

Chapter Thirteen

A cold night loomed. Dampness inside the van made the frigid air drive into his bones. The slightest movement touched off a series of chills that felt colder and sank deeper as the night wound on. He wiped away the condensation on the window. "That damn broad," he cursed under his breath. He was here because she had kept him from getting the papers. One mistake and he's forced to take chances like this. He held the coffee cup with both hands seeking its warmth. Inside the lunch bag he brought were two sandwiches. "Damn broad," he swore. He'd been watching the apartment for forty minutes now. The apartment was too well lit from the front, not unexpected but not ideal. He would try to get in through the back door again.

The food and drink settled his nerves. Breaking into an apartment was always nerve wracking. He was much more interested in outdoor events. He could plan his escape better, he could move, he could think on his feet. An apartment was a trap.

He took another long look around. There several buildings on a few acres of land, lots of plants along the periphery. The property had access to the parking lot by two streets and sidewalks in front of and around the buildings. Fortunately two of the street lights were burned out, he counted that in his favor. He decided to give himself ten minutes of observation then do the job. It was time to get his paperwork and get out of here. He looked for activity in the windows of the apartments. Most were dark. He saw a light flash up above one of the windows. Bats or some squirrel gathering nuts. He kept his eyes trained on the slats and waited. Another glint of light.

"That's gotta be someone," he said. "What's going on around here anyway?" Someone was spying. Voyeur, he thought, amateur.

"There's no way I can get in until that moron leaves." He'd better wait. Another night would be best, less exposure, fewer chances of getting caught. Losing those papers was costing him lots of time and energy.

He started up the van and drove away. He didn't turn his lights on until he made his first turn. He kept to the speed limit and cursed himself for being so lame a few nights ago. A late delivery to the Hotel Newsome: three cases of cleaning supplies, several boxes of retail items for the hotel store and a case of soaps, shampoos, conditioners for the guests.

Done for the night, he changed his clothes in the van and went in for a drink. In the hotel bar he listened to the music and enjoyed a few brews. If he hadn't been so far gone when he went to pay his tab, maybe he wouldn't have slipped up and left those receipts. He should have shredded them right after he got them. Too much haste makes too much waste. Why did that chick pick up those papers anyway? It all came down to sloppiness. Relaxing makes me sloppy, sloppiness makes me stupid, stupid makes me angry, anger has to be fixed. So I fixed the problem. She's not around and now I have to get those stupid papers back and destroy them.

He slammed his fist on the steering wheel and swore again. He over corrected his steering and just missed the trash can as he drove into his driveway. The house was in a blue collar part of town. It was weathered and unkempt. A low chain link fence rimmed the property, but was in places obscured by bushes. Windows not covered by overgrown rhododendrons outside were obscured by lace curtains inside that were tattered and faded.

Tonight, light passed through the living room curtain. From the van he saw the family portraits light up in blue flashes, he knew his mother was up, probably asleep in front of the TV again. He drove up to the garage. As the garage door rattled open an old AMC Rambler Six came into view. Several boxes sat on top of the car, bags littered the area around the car and dust held it all together. A narrow path through the junk was the only sign of recent activity. The car hadn't been driven for years. He entered the house through the garage.

"So, you're finally home," said his mother from the other room.

"Yeah, I finished up late tonight. You, okay, Ma?" he moved into the doorway. His mother was wrapped up in a multicolored knit blanket. Dressed for bed, she dangled a remote control from one hand and with the other gripped the wooden arm rest of the chair tightly.

"I can't sleep. I never can sleep. Are you okay?"

"I'm good. I'm starting early tomorrow. Gonna head to bed."

"You're not causing problems at work are you? When people have to work late that tells me they're not toeing the line. Are you using their time wisely? You sure you're keeping up? You can tell me."

"It's just busy right now, Ma. I'm doing my job." He headed down into the basement. Those stupid receipts had his address and phone number on them. Idiot. Now the only way to get the stuff back was steal it...maybe there was a simpler way to solve this problem. He smiled. Simpler is better. He needed to take advantage of his natural talent and do what he did best.

The morning sun broke through the cloud cover. A gentle breeze pushed against the small weeping willow outside the North Glendon Police Station. Madison heard the breeze move through the leaves and saw branches beat against the window as he walked to the door.

The computer screen on Madison's desk displayed the graphic version of the North Glendon Department of

Public Safety. He got up and walked out to Detective DeBrough's cubicle. It was empty.

"He's out on an interview. He should be back soon." Detective Korman leaned back in his seat. "How's De LaFleur going for you?"

"I've got two autopsy reports. They both have undetermined cause of death. De LaFleur had no physical signs of abuse. Clemons had abrasions from his fall, but nothing that would account for his death. He seems to have been dead before he hit the ground. And I'm still waiting for both tox reports."

"De LaFleur had bits of dirt and some miscellaneous debris that matched the area she was found in. She also had a powder of some kind on her, sort of like a body powder, but the ME isn't thinking drugs. It's being tested for composition and won't be back for a few weeks. Background checks don't tie them together. De LaFleur is from the Midwest and Clemons is from California. Their families say they can't think of any reason for either of them to be in trouble. No histories of early illness. Neither of them was into drugs. The only thing I see in common is they both were associated with the Hotel Newsome."

"Anyone see them hang out together? Maybe seeing each other outside of work?" said Korman.

"Not recently. They dated some time ago, but no one witnessed them together in the last few months. She was a waitress, he played in the band. They didn't always work the same shift. No one saw them as particularly friendly to each other. No known disagreements.

"What doesn't add up for me," Madison said, "is that her death takes place on the university campus and no one is around, no witnesses. I don't see how someone so young could die without some indication of why. Right now I think she was murdered, but I can't currently back it up."

"You'll probably know from the tox report."

"Yes. But I don't think I have time for that. With Clemons' death, I'm wondering about a serial killer. This sort of thing doesn't happen without cause."

"You better be sure on that. The politicos don't want to hear about that ever. Especially here in North Glendon."

"I know. And the Chief is starting to get pressure from them already."

"I don't suppose there's a new drug out that we're looking at? Maybe a new type of overdose?

"Not from what I can tell. That should have shown up in the autopsy if that were true."

"Okay. So are you thinking she actually died at another location? Then was transported here?"

"Either that, or someone killed her very quietly, somehow. Also, the M.E. noted that she had pierced ears but no earrings were found with the body. Do women with pierced ears go out without earrings?"

Korman shrugged. "I wouldn't think so, I don't think my wife ever does."

"And back to the body location, she was known to walk home at night, but no one knew if she had a specific route she took. The guy who found the body, Jeffrey Grant, says he didn't know she walked the same way he did. He had never seen her before in his walk home."

"Well, do you think he's good for it?"

"Hard to tell, I've got inquiries about his time in California. He's got a sealed juvenile record that I'm trying to get opened. He was divorced a while ago, not originally from California, but no recent criminal history. At the crime scene his were the only shoe prints found. Close to the body the trampled grass could show he moved her body. Something he didn't tell us when I talked to him."

"Any reason to think it wasn't an unexplained death and not murder?" said Korman.

"If all we had was her death, I would consider it. Clemons death and the tie to the Newsome suggests otherwise. Add in the 'unknown causes' from the autopsy and I think we're looking at a murder case. I also keep thinking there's got to be a legitimate cause of death. I've asked for additional tox screens just to eliminate a few things, but I don't even know what to suspect. It could be a wild goose chase for the lab."

"Look," Korman said, "The direction I'd go is deeper into the Newsome connection. Something will come out, it's just going to take more time than you'd like."

"I know. There's a lot of ways to go with that hotel and I was hoping to wrap this up before Bonnie got back."

"When's she due?"

"Monday. I don't remember a case like this before."

"Do you remember eight years ago when the suicides started at the university? The first one was straight forward, pills were found, some in the vics system, but it took the second suicide to find that obscure drug that was common to both cases." Korman was would up now and went on. "Then the Stuart Miller case. He was a student with a chemistry degree and pharmacy background. The prosecutor told me the kid was a narcissist. He acted normal at the trial, but in interviews before the trial everything was about him. The guy didn't react to causing pain in others, just viewed it all in relationship to how it affected him."

"I wonder if that's a connection I could make here. That's going to be tough to figure out without a perp." Madison leaned back into the chair. He thought about the missing earrings from De LaFleur and wondered if there was anything missing from Clemons. "I think I need to talk to those guys in the band again.

"Thanks for the talk, Korman. At times it's good to think out loud."

"Glad to help." He glanced at the clock. "I've got to meet DeBrough out front, see you later."

"According to the ME, Clemons was wearing a watch, black band with a chrome faceplate, and two rings. One ring had a gold band with initials on it and the other was gold with a school logo and a small garnet in green. Did he wear other jewelry you might know about?" said Madison.

Grant and Webb sat across the table in the Jazz Room. It was early evening and a few customers were finishing off dinners. The lights hadn't been dimmed for the evening crowd. Jeffrey had let the seltzer water sit while they talked. Madison had the impression Jeffrey and Harmon had been having an argument before he arrived. A look at the stage showed the drum kit had been righted and the pieces been pushed together.

Harmon was the first to answer. "I don't remember noticing him wear anything like jewelry. I don't even remember the two rings. Were they on opposite hands or both on the same?"

"I don't know," Madison said, "I'd have to look at the pictures."

Jeffrey said, "I think he sometimes wore a silver bracelet. It was about half an inch wide, on his right wrist. It had a design on it, hash marks and shapes. He told me it reminded him of a friend from his college days." Jeffrey shifted in his chair. "I couldn't tell you if he had it on when he died."

Madison made notes then pulled out the inventory list of Clemons items from the ME's office.

"There was a metal object shaped like a 't' in one of his pockets. It had a receptacle for a bolt or something on one end. Any ideas what that would be?" he asked.

Harmon snorted. "A drum key," he said. "He would use it to 'tune' his drums."

"Bill was always adjusting the tension on the drum heads, he'd spend thirty minutes before we started each night testing them out, getting the right pitch. He said the temperature and humidity affected the tones he'd get. I suppose he was right, he was good," said Jeffrey

"All right," said Madison. "What made you decide to start up tonight, why not wait for a few more days, maybe after the funeral?"

"The manager here said he was OK if we took few more days off, I'd rather we played. The routine helps."

"So it's just the two of you?"

"Harmon and I were figuring that out before you came over."

"Jeffrey, did you argue with Clemons?"

"I guess it looks bad because I found Sharon and now Bill."

"Of course he did," said Harmon.

"Artistic differences, Harmon, you know that," said Jeffrey.

"Not about Sharon, it wasn't."

"You don't know anything." He leaned in to Harmon. Jeffrey gripped the arms of the chair and his knuckles turned white.

"You and De LaFleur?" said Madison. "I thought that didn't work out."

"Clemons had peculiar interests with women. I didn't think it was right."

"What's peculiar?"

"He was aggressive."

"How?"

"This doesn't need to get out, right?"

"Depends on its relevance to the case."

"Who decides that? You?"

"Me to start with. If it takes me on the wrong path then it stops."

"Bill Clemons shouldn't be remembered for his peccadilloes."

"If it's not relevant, it gets dropped. What was his problem?"

"Asphyxiation. He told me recently that he'd met women who found it erotic."

Harmon Webb snorted. "Sick bastard," he said.

"We'd gotten drunk one night, maybe a month ago," said Jeffrey.

"All of you?" said Madison.

"Yeah. New contract with a little pay hike and a bonus," said Harmon.

"You do this often?" said Madison.

"First time since we started a few years back. We promised never to play drunk, two drink limit," said Jeffrey.

"Why?"

"Musicians have problems with excess. It's a cliché and it's true."

"What happened?"

"Manager gave us cash to seal the deal. We finished the night and headed over to Bills' apartment. He got maudlin, then excited. We all became like teenagers and told tall tales of our exploits. It was pathetic."

"You and Clemons confessed, I didn't," said Harmon.

"You told us all about your..."

"We were all drunk, you idiot." Harmon slammed his fist into the table.

"You were there," said Jeffrey.

"I passed out."

"Later in the night. You and Clemons were buddies at first."

"Can it, Jeffrey." Harmon got up and walked away from the table.

Madison and Jeffrey watched him go.

"So you tell me," said Madison.

"That's why Sharon dropped Bill. He wanted rough sex, she didn't. End of story. She was not a pushover."

Madison called the station as soon as he left the Newsome Hotel.

"I need more background on William Clemons. See if you can find out details about his early history in California. Let's get an interview with Sharon's family. She doesn't look like Snow White anymore. Any updates for me?"

He listened then hung up. Still no trace of the earrings, he thought. They could be a dead end, but Madison didn't think so yet. He also needed to find out more about this serial killer thread.

Chapter Fourteen

A cat moved deliberately through the tall grass, low, slow, and stealthy. It was a thin creature that stalked its prey with care. In the darkness, the feline was well hidden among the stems of weeds and grass. As she moved close to the abandoned house her line of travel shifted and she startled. Carolyn stepped quietly out of the shadows and into the path at the far side of the property. She walked to the back door of the house and let herself in.

Nothing had been moved. The thread near the floor was still in place. The cheesecloth across the doorway to the kitchen hadn't been moved. She breathed a deep sigh and felt herself relax.

She counted three shirts and a pair of jeans that were clean. She would need more clothing if she was going to stay here long. She had been so focused on finding the papers in the apartment she neglected longer term needs. What a mistake. A nice warm shower was also overdue, but that would have to wait. She was tapped out. Fortunately she was paid up at the apartment through the end of the month. If it felt safe later, she could go back.

She hoped this mess would be worked through by then and she could return to a normal life.

Camping out wasn't new for her. Her brother, Dan, had become her mentor after her mother's death. He was an outdoors man. A few years older than Carolyn, he liked having her along on his trips. Carolyn remembered how he had watched her so patiently as she started her first campfire. Both of them had been damp and cold from an early rain. The kindling was a mix of pine needles and branches in early decay. Piled in a teepee shape, it should have been easy to get the fire started with the flint and ignitor. After a dozen swipes with not enough spark to generate a flame the needles finally caught and flamed up.

A few years later Dan received the cancer diagnosis and then passed away within months. Carolyn withdrew. She sought solace in the hills and trails where she and Dan had spent so much time. The forest became a safe and sane haven when grief threatened to quench her spirit.

Now as she prepared to engage her mind to survive against an unknown enemy, Carolyn felt bitterness melt into her body. She hated being driven into hiding. She hated the fear that was welling up in her. She slammed a cup to the floor, the sound blasted across the room.

After taking another deep breath she began to think. Why was that receipt for chemicals so important to Sharon? Or was it? Who needed it so badly they would kill for it?

She would get over to the library and do some research in the morning. She heard the sound of a scratch against wood. Carolyn looked for a weapon. She picked up a board from the floor and steadied herself for a blow. Mewling sounded on the far side of the room. A paw and then the body of the tabby she'd seen earlier entered the room. The cat took a sniff at the stove and then sat to watch Carolyn.

Carolyn considered the cat. Her arrival might mean other guests would be arriving. Then again, the cat could eliminate unwanted rodents and be a sort of alarm system for her. She sat down on the bed and dropped her head in her hands. A wave of fear ran through her, she calmed and then took a deep breath. A cleansing breath, as a yoga instructor had once said over and over through classes. Carolyn recognized the emotion she felt as a combination of exhaustion from running away, fear of the unknown man, and a lack of time talking with someone she trusted.

Sharon De LaFleur had filled that role at times. They weren't friends, but over time they had reached an agreement about getting together to talk. Morning coffee, sometimes evening conversations with the television murmuring low in front of them, some weekend late night sessions after both arrived home from work. She knew she was feeling the burden of loss. She felt the loss of Sharon, loss of home, loss of security.

Even the thought of returning to work with the students brought her chills. Maybe her attacker, stalker was one of them. Her strength seemed to be ebbing away, her resolve became quiet, subdued, listless. Carolyn closed her eyes and for a few minutes gave in to the feeling of loss, a tear moved down her cheek.

She sat up and straightened her shoulders. Her slow breathing became sure and faster. Finally, she opened her eyes to the light of her makeshift room, looked at the warm glow of the lamp, then allowed her shoulders to drop back to a normal position, all her tension gone. Would she be able to find peace in her life again? When would she be able to make a new home for herself? What about companionship? She got up and continued preparing her dinner. Carolyn noticed the cat wasn't in a hurry to leave. She decided to ignore the animal and see what happened. Perhaps the best way to deal with an intruder like this is just to let them be, let them seek and find nothing and then move on. She tried to remember what she'd learned about animals with her brother. Mostly she remembered that they were independent cusses.

After carefully surveying each other, pretending to ignore each other, and finally accepting their situation, they settled into silence and acceptance. They needed each other.

Chapter Fifteen

Today, day five of the investigation, was moving day. Madison collected the file on the case and reorganized the paperwork. He forced himself to reexamine the evidence. He, at this point, presumed that Sharon De LaFleur was murdered. Even without a known cause he felt the lack of a natural cause of death was enough to suggest homicide. Combined with the equally suspicious death of William Clemons, Madison was confident he was right. The looming questions revolved around determining if the murderer, if there was only one, was a serial killer or if, in fact, there were multiple killers. He suspected a single killer using the same M.O. with an unknown motive. Little information of importance had surfaced at the Newsome with those interviews. It was time to dig deeper on another path. First he would check out the background of De LaFleur.

Madison picked up the transcription from the interview conducted with Sharon's mother, Molly De LaFleur. The interview had been done at Molly's home in Cold Spring, Minnesota. Detective Jennifer Hoppe received Madison's emailed questions and asked other questions as the interview progressed.

Molly told Hoppe that Sharon was rebellious. She had called them all "religious hypocrites." School records reflected numerous citations for arguing and fighting with the teachers. "Hard headed from day one, and made up excuses to keep away from Sunday school, too," quoted Hoppe in her report. The family was religious and kept a tight rein on the girls. George De LaFleur was pictured with a white shirt and tie, and wearing a dark jacket. Detective Hoppe concluded that Sharon had been shunned by the family after she ran away at the age of seventeen. Molly wasn't sure where she had lived and "Her being dead doesn't come as a surprise to me, may God bless her soul." Hoppe gained access to Sharon's juvenile records and discovered three instances of arrest for theft. Convicted of forgery and possession of controlled substances, Sharon had served time at a juvenile facility and then released with community service hours.

Madison closed out the report, and took another look at the particulars of the murder. The next call he got came from the Chief Stanton. He was being summoned to her office.

"So, what's the latest, Madison?" Stanton said. "Just give me the update."

"First blush looks like two homicides with no obvious connections."

"The city council is having an event at the Newsome hotel in a week. I've been getting questions about these incidents. They don't want an unsolved murder associated with the place."

"Me either," Madison said. Urgency on the PD's part in solving the murder at the Newsome Hotel was always a priority. "What does that mean to me?" he said.

"I'm giving you some help. You okay with Riggs and Smart? They'll have to split shifts to keep their regular areas covered."

"Of course, I'll take it. You know my partner is due back on Tuesday, that's another hand for the crew."

"She'll be picking up your other cases and finishing up reports until the end of Thursday."

"I was hoping she'd get going on the De LaFleur and Clemons case."

"I don't have time, nor do I want to discuss this with you. Work this out, use Riggs and Smart, get the evidence right, and do it by Friday. I've seen the other reports, seen the photos, it looks straight forward, just don't screw it up. Whoever did this is not smart enough to hide and clean up everything. Keep me in the loop."

"Okay."

"It's not you," she said, "People in town would love to use this as an example of my incompetence. I'm not going to let them do it. This fell into your lap, you've worked with less and handled it well, do it again, just faster. Now get out of here, I've got calls to make."

It's starting to hit the fan and it's early in the investigation. It's too bad for me and too bad for the DA. There goes my sleep cycle.

"Right, Chief," he said. The door slammed behind him.

In his office, Madison picked up his review of the evidence. Detective DeBrough walked in.

"I've got Bonnie Cho on the line. She's one of the waiters at the Newsome. She remembers the earrings."

"Get her info and let's talk to her now," said Madison.

Chapter Sixteen

A chill wind settled into the air as Carolyn made her second journey back to the apartment that same night. Rain swirled close as she walked and dampness seeped into her bones. She shivered and tried to think clearly. Her quest for rain gear superseded her sense of safety. The pools of light along the street became targets she needed to miss. Light had become an enemy that put her at risk from whoever had stalked her last night. What could she expect when she arrived? Who was it stalking her? Why the violence? Why now? What exactly had happened? For so long she had kept a low profile and no one had interfered. Everything had been going well. Until now.

As she made her way through the shadows her steps rang in her ears. Another block closer and she began to feel tense. The rain had settled into a swirling mist. Someone was near her, lingering, unhealthy, malevolent. Her chills increased, she stopped, listened, her breath slowed, her hearing became tuned to the night. A scurry of tiny feet, drops of water hitting pavement, a slight whistle of air through branches. Where was the presence now? Gone? It had moved away. It wasn't totally gone, but she felt a little lighter, buoyed by the change. The odor of earth and decaying leaves came and went with the breeze. The danger had abated no more presence of evil. She picked up her pace and walked to the apartment.

Across from her building, Carolyn paused in the shadow of a tree. The chill air kept her alert, but she could feel the energy drain from her. Her way seemed clear. She made her move and walked to the back door of her apartment. Inside, she went to her room for a bag and some clothes.

After drinking too many beers, Barry Green had fallen asleep in the attic. At one o'clock in the morning he woke to a sour taste in his mouth and movement in his stomach. He had a cramp in his calf that demanded immediate attention. His father had always called them charley horses, but all Barry cared about was the pain. He climbed down to the bathroom to relieve himself. No more beers for him tonight.

He settled back into his attic perch and picked up the binoculars. He saw light in the De LaFleur apartment. They're back, he thought. Should he surprise them or call the cops himself? He made two decisions that seemed right at the time. One, he called 911 and got an immediate response, they were on their way. Two, he wanted to be in on the action for this one.

Barry met up with the police at the apartment when they arrived, but the police thought he was the burglar and cuffed him. In his inebriated state he began screaming at the officers and they added resisting arrest to the charges. In the back seat of the patrol car, Barry couldn't produce ID for the officers and they willingly went in to his apartment to find his wallet. They found the open staircase leading to his voyeurs' perch. And they found an open cardboard box of contraband from his forays into apartments over the years. Barry had neatly labeled the date and apartment number of every item in the box. Within and hour a warrant appeared and Barry discovered the fruits of his 911 call would lead to his own re-incarceration at the city jail until his arraignment.

Carolyn gathered two bags of clothes from drawers and closets and stacked them by the back door. She went into Sharon's room to see if she had missed anything. Someone had been through the room. The dresser drawers stuck out randomly. An end table by the bed was shifted away and crooked. Carolyn knew Sharon wasn't meticulous about her room, but neither was she careless. Another look at the shelf of books and ten minutes spent pulling them from the shelves and fanning them upside down revealed nothing new.

She heard the siren and doused the light. Then she left the apartment. Across the short distance of the back lawn she dropped into a thicket of bushes.

The light show from the police car made the scene carnival-like as Carolyn peered around the corner. By now, several neighbors had formed a crowd outside.

Officer's voices mixed with Barry's screams. Two more police cars arrived, the crowd grew, and the flashing lights and the scratchy voices on walkie talkies was like an episode of "Cops" in super high definition. Carolyn couldn't figure out what was happening, but decided not to wait to be discovered.

The phone rang several times before Madison was roused out of a heavy sleep. "Madison," he said. A long pause and then he rolled out of bed. "I'll meet them there. Ten minutes." He dressed, splashed water on his face and drove to Sharon De LaFleurs apartment.

"Who's running this one," he asked.

"Ferrin's leading, she was first to arrive," an officer said. "She's getting a statement from the perp now."

The perp's shouts died down. He was running out of steam. Ferrin shook her head and tucked the notepad away in her pocket. Madison stayed back a step and waited for the exchange to end.

"Detective," she said.

"Who is this guy, and what's he got to do with the De LaFleur case?"

In the car, Barry Green was twitching and mumbling to himself.

"Looks like we've got a voyeur," Ferrin said. "He called in a disturbance. When we arrived, Mr. Green smelled of alcohol and insisted on grabbing the burglar in De LaFleurs' apartment. He wouldn't calm down so my partner went to check out the apartment. Mr. Green interfered. He started yelling about seeing a flash of light in the apartment from his place. The problem is, from his place you can't see into the apartment. You've gotta be up a story, in the attic, looking through those vents." she pointed to the building where Green lived.

"We asked and were given the grand tour of his place so we could see what he did. I think he's drunk enough that he forgot it's wrong to stare at people through windows. A quick visual of Mr. Green's apartment was enough to get the search warrant. He's got a regular crow's nest up there, chair, ice chest, a twenty-two with a scope, a box of goods stolen from other apartments. The Chief said I should call you right away, so here you are," she said.

Madison nodded, "You're right about that. He's an ex-con, right?"

"I called for his record, we'll know soon."

Crime scene investigators inside the apartment were doing a thorough job of ferreting out the intimate details of Barry Green's life. Few drawers remained untouched. Many were empty. If anything here pointed to him as the murderer, they'd find it.

"Isn't this guy the maintenance man here?" he asked.

"Doesn't look like a really organized guy, though," an officer said. "Everything is in piles. Even paperwork looks like it's been left where it was read."

From experience Madison knew killers, those who didn't kill family, coworkers or lovers, tended to be neat, often obsessively so. The mess here didn't follow that pattern. The mess was just a mess, the reflection of a jumbled mind working on impulse.

"How do I get into the attic?" he said.

The officer, Mullins it said on his badge, pointed to the bedroom. A flow of air came from the closet in the back. A ladder led up to the hole cut into the ceiling. An officer was snapping pictures of the attic.

"Take a look out the air vent. No one's been here to dust yet, but if you stay in the center you'll be good," the officer said.

Madison approached the eve and looked through the slats. A clear shot to the De LaFleur apartment. The patrol car lights added an odd effect to the feel of the room, as though the colors were reaching in and touching everything for a moment. I don't think Mr. Green wanted to end his day this way. His hobby exposed, his freedom gone, his life altered way beyond expectation.

"Let me know if you guys find anything," he said to Mullins on the way out.

Mullins said, "Is there something I should look for?"

"I don't know yet. Maybe some sort of unusual drugs, prescription or unlabeled. I'd look for plants that you can't easily identify. Or even chemicals with odd names, plant food or something."

"That's gonna be in his tool shed, if there is anything." Mullins gave an order to one of the other officers. "Probably won't have an inventory until late in the day."

"Make it sooner," said Madison.

"Yes, sir."

Madison approached Ferrin at the patrol car.

"I'd like to take a look at the De LaFleur place," he said.

"It doesn't look like it was touched," she replied.

"Do you think someone was here?"

"I don't know."

Madison's phone rang.

"What's up? Carolyn Pendle? I know. She's missing. Okay. I'll be there soon."

"Did they find her?" said Ferrin.

"No. Someone has filed a missing person report. They're at the station now. Looks like no more rest tonight."

The night air felt good to him. He really enjoyed the invigorating feel of a cold night. When he got warm, he got sleepy. When he was comfortable and cozy, his defenses were down. That never ended well. He remembered the first time he was seduced by comfort. He had been a kid working, trying to get a few bucks washing dishes at a diner. They were helping him out, getting him started at a career. He had worked long hours for low pay. One night he fell asleep sitting on a bucket in the back corner of the restaurant. When the cook found him he had thrown a knife into the wall near his head. Startled awake he had nearly given himself a concussion when he slammed his head into the counter. He had been fired and afraid.

The sound of his tires on the wet streets cut in and out of his mind as he drove. The wind swirling around him, the lights flashing by, the unsteady water whooshing to an orchestral arrangement that filled his mind like a movie that he watched, felt, lived in, but wasn't real. He knew the things he thought he might have done probably weren't real, they were the warm and cozy part of life that never worked out for him. Even tonight as he neared the apartment to clean up the mess of his negligence, he wondered what part of it was real.

He could see the lights well before he arrived. It was the red and blue flashes that were a staple of so many idiotic TV shows. Damn, he said to himself. Now what. He slowed the van and slid into a shadow by the street. He couldn't remain hidden this way, a white van at night still attracts light. He was anonymous in the day but at night the van became a conduit for light. He shut off the van. From his vantage point, he could see he wasn't going to get to the apartment tonight. That idiot at the apartment done has done something. He slammed the heel of his hand into the steering wheel and cursed to himself. Somewhere in the apartment is the only evidence that connects me to a murder and it's surrounded by cops.

From disappointment he moved to ill humor and then on to anger in the space of a minute. His own temper kept him warm even as the night wind picked up and began to infiltrate the cargo van. The metal creaked now and again as the interior cooled. Eddie tapped his foot against the carpet and silently seethed. He gave the steering wheel a death grip. All the tension of the night crescendoed into a roar as he released a growl from within that rocked the van. From outside he looked like he was convulsing, the yell became a low grumble and his face was puffed up and savage. No one was witness to his tantrum. He knew it was time to leave. He took several deep breaths, slammed his hand into the steering wheel again, then started up the van and left.

Chapter Seventeen

When he arrived at the office, Dr. Winslows' final autopsy report on Sharon De LeFleur was the first thing Madison opened. De LaFleur died of a heart attack. Her heart was working then it stopped. The tox screening would tell them what enzymes were affected and if there were abnormal chemical events that took place. Traces of other chemicals would not be available for two weeks. There were no indications of other types of injury except what might happen from a fall. No sexual penetration, no ligature marks, not even defense wounds, no indications of a reason for her to have died. Madison called Dr. Winslow.

"Doc?" he said. "I read the report. Two weeks for the tox screening?"

"Unless I can get the lab to move it to the top of the list, that's it. I told them it's a murder case."

"If William Clemons report is the same as De LaFleur we may have a serial killer."

"Do you think it's going that way? I haven't got the final done for Clemons yet."

"I don't want to risk waiting. If you can push the lab please do it. Otherwise, I'll have to get the Chief involved and that immediately becomes political. Nothing has been said officially, yet."

"Let me make a call to Solomon, he's head of the crime lab and he owes me a favor."

"If you need back up, let me know. And let's only tell those who need to know. This is an inquiry that could lead to panic if it gets public."

"Okay, Madison. I understand. I hope you're wrong."

As he hung up, Madison told himself he wanted to be wrong. A knock came at the door and Officer Ferrin stepped in. She looked as haggard as he felt and likely hadn't gotten off shift since he last saw her.

"I haven't written it up yet but thought you might want to know," she said.

"What's that, Ferrin?"

"It looks like the roommate of De LaFleur was at the apartment last night," she sat down in the chair. "Several of the witnesses saw the same light Mr. Green reported."

"I thought he was making it up."

"So did I. Her neighbor said the other woman was Carol Pendle, she worked somewhere at the University. Didn't socialize much, but hasn't been seen since De LaFleur died. The neighbor, Leona Smoza, heard a crash at the apartment the night of De LaFleur's death. She didn't want to appear nosy so she ignored it. But she did wonder why the apartment was empty for the last few nights."

"So we've got a name, that's good," he said. He picked up the phone. "Sargeant, put out an APB for a Carolyn Pendle, I'll send you the last known address."

Ferrin stood and waited while he made the call.

"I'm interested in moving to homicide and sex crimes," she said.

"The Chief makes that call, but I can put in a word."

"Thanks. Appreciate the opportunity."

A records check for Carolyn Pendle showed fingerprints and a gun permit. Reason for the permit was to be eligible to carry for the university security patrol. The gun permit was not required for the job, but it was not an unusual request.

His thoughts turned back to the investigation, to Carolyn Pendle, to the mystery of why De LaFleur had died.

"Good night, Mrs. Henson," said Jeffrey Grant. He locked the front door and walked away.

"Mr. Grant," she said.

Widowed and in her late seventies, Mrs. Henson kept careful watch of the activities in the neighborhood. She knew the neighborhood well and had given him an exhaustive rundown of its life and times shortly after he moved in. In the course of two months, eight cups of tea and numerous scones in her half of the duplex, she had told young Jeff—Jeffrey seemed a little pretentious—that he would be an acceptable neighbor. He had explained that he worked odd hours and she assured him she would watch out for him.

From a distance, someone looking at Jeffrey walk away from the house might have thought him drunk. He would take an off stride step at times, and on the times he did look up could be heard humming or lip syncing to some tune that didn't sound melodic. Up close, he was ruminating. He thought about the discovery of Sharon, the loss of his friend Bill Clemons at the Newsome, the interrogations he had undergone, and knowing he was a suspect in Sharon's death, maybe even Clemons'.

If he looked at it rationally, dispassionately, he came to the same conclusions that Detective Madison came up with. He had been there, he found her, and he knew her. It was almost as though he had been set up. But why? Who would gain from Sharon's death, who would even want to set him up as the murderer? Questions floated around in his mind as he considered and reconsidered the scenarios. It all seemed random to him. And then to have Bill die in the way he did. Then again, Jeffrey wondered if their deaths were related, but he couldn't figure out how.

She worked at the Newsome, he thought, so did Bill. They were of necessity night owls. As far as he knew, they weren't involved. But then, would he really know about that? His knowledge of Sharon was shallow, just the odd hello, how are you and goodbye at night. He knew Bill better. But again, their relationship was about the music. Bill had quit drinking after his college years, Jeffrey had given up his alcoholic binges after an incident years earlier that threw him into adulthood fifteen years after most others had gotten there.

What linked the deaths of Sharon and Bill? He would have to do some digging on his own. He would have to clear himself where the evidence was against him.

The evening sky took on a blue hue. As leaves began their short journey from branch to ground, a northern chill settled in as the sun fell to the horizon. For the first time in a several weeks, rain didn't fall on Jeffrey as he walked. Without thinking, he walked to the Newsome. At the hotel he passed by people, nodded and made the appropriate noises as they walked by, but he was not there.

On stage he picked up his guitar and wondered if the murders were in any way tied to the theft of his other guitar. He might mention that to the police the next time he talked with them. In his mind both Sharon and Bill were murdered, Detective Madison hadn't said that, but Jeffrey presumed it since he was under suspicion.

A light crowd dined tonight. The sounds of silverware on plates acted like a carpet of audio low and underfoot. Jeffrey went to the bar.

"Soda water on the rocks," Jeffery said.

Barlow said, "You're here early."

"I just couldn't stay away," he said.

"Right, like you're gonna own the place soon?" he replied. "Not as a musician, you're not." He placed a cardboard coaster on the bar and sat down the drink.

Waitresses moved around collecting glasses, depositing trays, making change and swiping plastic through electronic readers. Business began to pick up. Barlow moved down the bar, filled a few orders and cleaned glasses. When he moved closer Jeffrey got his attention.

"Did you notice any action between Sharon and Bill?"

"You're sounding like those cops," he said. "They asked the same thing the other night after Bill died."

"You know I'm a suspect. I have connections to both of them, and I guess loose alibis for both."

"I never thought about it, but you're right. I'll bet they're really digging into your history by now." The grin came back on his face. "At least, I'm not high on their list."

"What makes you think that? You knew them both, aside from the issue of Sharon's death, you could have done it as much as me."

"You think?"

"Sure, I wouldn't ignore someone like you. You dated Sharon didn't you?"

"We went out a couple times. We were not compatible, different interests outside of work, different tastes in music, even our politics didn't mesh. You know, she was looking for money, which I don't have."

"I didn't get the money interest from her. I never even dated her."

"She didn't shout it out, but it seemed important. After the second time out I wasn't on her list of eligible bachelors. Her attitude even put me off dating for a while. The detective was interested when I mentioned that."

Barlow headed down the bar. Jeffrey watched as the server read off a list of drinks. Barlow began pulling down glasses and grabbed bottles from the shelves. A glance at his phone told Jeffrey that he still had time before Harmon would arrive. When Barlow returned Jeffrey started in again.

"I've got a question for you." Jeffrey reached over the bar and helped himself to the fountain hose to refill his glass.

"I really didn't know Sharon," said Barlow.

"I know, but what about Clemons? Do you know if they ever went out?"

"Not recently. You guys have been playing here for over a year and I remember seeing them walk out a few times a while back. Probably last spring. Did they go out? I don't know."

"How did she seem to you when she was working?"

"She seemed a little put out last week. She told me she was pissed. I asked about what, and she just snorted and left."

"Okay."

"She was private, you know, she only talked to customers when she had to," he said. "She didn't say much to the rest of us really. I mean, everyone gets tense when things are busy, act a little pissy, but mostly we get through it. On down times, Sharon mostly talked about work and opinions about what was going on around here. You know management and things like that."

"Guess she talked to you a lot then."

"Now that you've got me thinking, she was talking about something different. Could have been the night she died. Maybe one of the girls would remember better. Posey is due in later. She was on that night, ask her."

"I will." Jeffrey refilled his soda and went back to the stage. Harmon Webb had arrived and was fiddling with the cords to the PA system.

"What's up, Harmon?" he said. Webb pulled at one of the plugs and gestured with it to Jeff.

"The other night all the commotion screwed up the wires. Then the cops came along and jumbled them some more." He shook his head and started unscrewing the connector end from the wire. Jeffrey wondered if Harmon was as indifferent to Bill's death at he seemed. Harmon's aloof manner was not feigned, he really didn't care most of the time.

"So what are you going to do, check both ends of all the wires to the PA?"

"No. All I've got to do is pull the wires for the mics from the drum kit, which eliminates three inputs right off. They will be gone, which means less mess."

"Taking his stuff already?" said Jeffrey.

"Look, the guy's gone, we can work like this for now, a week or two, then figure out what to do from there. I'm telling you, I didn't get on well with Bill. He was a nice guy, just not very interesting to talk to. You understand?"

"Why didn't I know you guys didn't get along?" he said.

"I avoided the guy, drummers are like that. My experience is the more you avoid them the better off you are. Bill butted into more conversations than anyone I know. Once he knew you'd let him talk, he couldn't resist jumping in. It was annoying."

Harmon began wrapping up one of the wires.

"I never noticed that," Jeffrey said. "Are you sure?"

"You don't notice lots," Webb said. "Last Saturday, Clemons butted right in when I was talking with Sharon De LaFleur. She was asking about a word she'd read, sounded like a chemical name, and Bill chimes in about trying an arrangement of a Basie tune or some idiotic thing like that. I didn't even know the guy was there." Harmon flipped a wrap around the wire and tossed it on top of another just like it.

"You're picking up Bill's mic?" Jeffrey asked. He reached over to grab it himself.

"Mine was acting funny, loose wires, a bad connector. I'm using his because it works. I didn't like him, he didn't get it, and I'm sorry he's dead. But I'm not going to get maudlin." Webb pulled the microphone back to himself.

Jeffrey stood up straight. He frowned as he gestured with his hands.

"What do you mean he didn't get it? He was the best local guy on the skins. You know it."

"He was always trying to overpower my solos." Harmon pushed a mic stand over.

Jeffrey jumped back as the stand hit the stage.

"Cut it out, you cur! This is expensive stuff."

"That's all you care about. You've got the biggest cut because it's your equipment. With Bill gone you're cut's going to be bigger."

"Who cares about the money?" Jeffrey pointed the mic at Harmon, shaking. "You're so selfish you can't even feel sympathy for Bill's death."

"You're right. He was your friend, not mine. I joined for the music not the company."

"So you want out?"

"No! I want to play. I want to drown myself in jazz and forget about the other eighteen hours of the day. Life stinks outside of here. I hate it."

There was a long silence. Jeffrey and Harmon noticed that the whole room was silent and staring at them. A lone figure was walking toward them briskly.

At the bar Gina Posey watched the action on the stage.

"I wondered what would happen tonight," said Gina.

"Death tests everyone who is left. No one is untouched," said Barlow. He cleaned glasses as he talked. "I don't like seeing it with friends."

"He seemed nice," she said. "I thought he tried to make a move on Sharon De LaFleur."

"You mean Bill?"

"Yes. Everyone thought it wouldn't pan out."

"Why?"

"She was independent. Quiet."

"So?"

"So Bill would have needed her to be a *girlfriend*. She didn't fit the role."

"You think Bill was needy?"

"Most men are."

"Ah." Barlow moved away to fill an order.

The manager strode up to the stage. His jacket was open and his tie hung loose.

"If you're done acting like children I'd like a word in the back room."

They walked single file.

"Your contract goes through the end of the month. If you don't want to fill it let me know. I'll make the call and find a band to fill the hole. I don't want either of you arguing like that again. That will be cause for termination of the contract."

"You're right," said Jeffrey.

"I know I'm right. This is a business. Clemons is gone. I don't want to hear about this again. Deal with it.

Tonight you will be here until closing. I'd like you to be professional about it. Tomorrow you can let me know about the rest of the month." He walked out of the room and closed the door.

"He's right," said Jeffrey again.

"I don't like it," said Harmon.

"Let's finish the gig tonight."

"I don't like people dying at work."

"Who would?"

"Same thing happened before when I played Serafinas' in Seattle."

"You mean that fire eight years ago?"

"Yeah. I don't like it. Let's play tonight. We'll talk tomorrow."

Chapter Eighteen

The night had gone well. Once the music started, Jeffrey and Harmon played like a tight jazz duo ought to. At the end of the night Jeffrey sat at the bar with Gina Posey.

"The night Sharon died I remember she and Bill were talking just before closing. It wasn't heated, just intense, you know how people gesture more and look out occasionally when they're conspiring. Well, that's the feeling I got when I saw them. It must have been good, whatever they were talking about," said Gina.

"Did they do that often? I don't remember seeing them ever talking."

"Not really. You knew they had gone out a few times, right? I even told the police all this stuff when Sharon died."

"Bill didn't say anything to me."

"Maybe he didn't tell you all he knew," said Gina. She picked up her purse and walked away.

"See you tomorrow."

"Maybe," said Jeffrey.

Madison read through the interviews with the Newsome staff again. He knew Sharon had gone out with several of the staff, including William Clemons. The picture he received was that she didn't care for the women much, but would talk with the men. Even so, most descriptions of her personality said she was distant. He decided he would go downtown tonight and follow up on a few details.

The white cargo van was parked by the Newsome Hotel. In the driver's seat, the man sat checking out his look for the night. Earlier he had gotten a haircut. This haircut made him look neater than his usual barber did. 'Casual business' was what he had asked for at the shop. Short on the sides, long enough to part on the right side, neatly trimmed edges, the guy did a good job, although he charged almost double what he expected. The button down shirt and slacks with loafers completed his look. Fishing for information was always tricky. Tonight he wanted the business attire to make him look innocuous. He slid on the black frame glasses with clear lenses and left the van.

The Jazz Room was full tonight. College kids out the night before classes start up and tourists at a trade show or an athletic event. He walked into the room. He shrugged off his jacket and was directed to a small table. He could hear the music, probably some modern tune, he thought. He didn't recognize the sound and, well, he probably wouldn't anyway. What was that jazz stuff to him?

A perky server came over and identified herself as Bonnie and asked, "What can I help you with?" he asked for black coffee and said he'd check out the menu.

As soon as she left he scoped out the room again. As the delivery guy he usually didn't pay much attention to the places he stopped in. Tonight, he needed to figure out if someone here had picked up his papers, or got them from the girl he killed. He knew the risk he took coming here tonight. He might be recognized as a witness to that girl's last night here. Bonnie returned and he ordered soup and a sandwich. After she left, he got up and went to the men's room. From there a stop at the bar seemed appropriate as he waited for his food.

"What can I get you?" asked Jim Barlow.

"Cream. I forgot to ask." Jim Barlow slid a container onto the counter. The man stayed with him. The bar guy didn't act like he recognized him, he thought. That's good.

"Ain't this the place where the lady was killed the other night, and then some musician died?" he asked.

"Sharon worked here but died over by the university. And the drummer with those guys on the stage died just a few days later. Bad news."

"I thought this was the place," he said. "Did you know the woman? I mean, you work here, maybe you saw something. I just was wondering if her friends were setting up some memorial thing or whatever."

"You know her?" asked Barlow.

"No. I'm just curious. This sort of thing doesn't happen every day."

"Not here."

"So you heard about a memorial?"

"Not me. Are you here for an event?"

"I leave tomorrow. Thanks for the cream." The man went back to the table and waited. When the server came back with his order, he tried again.

"You know the lady that was killed?"

"Sure. Sharon worked nights like most of us. Did you know her?" asked Bonnie.

"No. I'm curious about what happened. They didn't say much in the paper."

"I know. It's sad. She wasn't really social, you know. I don't think any of us knew her well."

"What do you think happened?"

"I can't think about it. Sorry, I've got to get back. If you need anything else let me know, okay?"

As Bonnie walked away, the man's face changed like a mask had been peeled off. His eyes went dead. His jaw tensed and relaxed. Without touching the soup he put money on the table and left the Newsome.

Madison walked over to the bartender, Jim Barlow. Madison introduced himself and took a seat.

"I know you've been interviewed but I have follow up questions. Did you know Sharon De LaFleur well?"

"Not me. I wouldn't say Sharon really had friends here."

"Why would that be?"

"I don't think she tried to make friends. Some people don't." Barlow let the sentence hang as he started filling glasses.

"Who do you think knew her best?"

"Who knew Sharon the best? I'd say Bill Clemons." Jim answered. "I told the other detective they went out, you know."

"I've read the report," Madison said. "What about since the interview. Have you remembered anything you think I should know?" Madison's phone rang. "It'll be here when? Okay. I'll look for it."

"Your phone going off reminds me. She did act funny the night before she died," Barlow said.

"What do you mean, funny?"

"I got a call when we were cleaning up. Someone was asking when we closed for the night. I told him we are closed and he cursed then rang off."

"What does that have to do with Sharon De LaFleur?"

"She was cleaning off the servers' part of the bar. I remember she started to ask me something, saw I was on the phone, then turned away and stuffed something in her pocket. I thought it was a tip."

"Wouldn't she normally collect her tips?"

"No, we pool tips here. I'd forgotten that incident until now. I wonder if it means anything."

"It might."

"That night she wiped down the bar, and kept humming some tune. I think it was 'I'm in the money.' A little odd, but she kept repeating it."

"What sort of jewelry did Sharon wear?"

"Jewelry? You might ask one of the servers. I don't really know." Barlow walked away.

Madison assumed the interview was over. He needed to get a look at the coroners' report for William Clemons. He would be back to pick up another interview later, maybe talk to a server. It's early but Madison was feeling tired. He needed sleep, a good meal, and solid answers. And he needed them sooner rather than later.

Outside, the streetlight illuminated the rain that had started to fall. Carolyn paused in the doorway of the building across from the Newsome Hotel. Standing in the shadows she once again considered the wisdom of what she was about to do. Whatever had happened at the Newsome cost Sharon her life. Now Carolyn had been drawn into the situation and needed to figure out why she had been attacked. Her attacker knew her, she didn't know him. Her intuition told her it had something to do with an incident here at the Newsome. She was tired of camping out at that old house. She was getting fearful and irritable, jumpy about noises and afraid she was being followed. She felt like it was time to stop running and engage.

While she wasn't dressed as inconspicuously as she'd have liked, her clothes were clean, the palazzos she wore might have been suited to a night of dancing, but the outfit was all she could find at Goodwill. She walked across the street and into the lobby of the Newsome Hotel.

Chapter Nineteen

E asy, clean guitar and piano played "Walkin' With Buddy" as Carolyn entered the room. The guitar solo mimicked the melody and felt like soothing soft notes tickling her ears. She stopped and took a survey of the room. The tables were lit by small electric lights with faux Tiffany shades. The lamps tossed a soft circle of light on the table cloths. The room was small enough to contain the pulsing of the eclectic jazz on stage, large enough to seat a hundred shadows at the tables where the sound food and drink could be heard. She stepped up to the sign that welcomed guests. A server tagged "Bonnie" on her badge, escorted her to a table across the room.

"Are you looking for dinner? We close up the kitchen in half an hour," the server said. "Something light, a sandwich, and coffee," Carolyn said.

The music faded out, lights on the stage dimmed. The musicians were taking a break. Now that she was here, she wasn't so sure she should have come. A cup of coffee appeared on the table.

"I didn't mean to scare you," said Bonnie.

"That's all right. Can I ask you a question?"

Bonnie nodded.

"Did you know Sharon?"

"Sure. We all did. Who are you?"

"She was my roommate. I'm Carolyn."

"It's so sad that she died, I hope they figure out what happened. It's kind of creepy not knowing."

"I'm wondering if you knew her, or who here might have known her well."

"I would think you knew her best."

"She didn't talk much."

"She was a loner here, too."

"Do you know if she was friends with any of the guys? I know she stayed out sometimes, but she wouldn't talk to me about it."

Bonnie hesitated. "Sharon was rude like that."

"Look, I've been attacked and followed for the last two days. I'm trying to find out what's going on here. Give me something to go on." She slapped the table.

"I've told everything I know to the police. If you want more information try the bartender, he knows everyone."

Carolyn became distracted by an argument taking place between the bartender and a customer. A drunk most likely, she thought. The man in a blazer and slacks flung up his arms up as though conducting a concerto. The bartender planted his hands on the bar and nodded while he listened to the rant. Another man further down the bar stared at the ranter and froze. Whatever the incident was, people would glance over, then turn back to their meals. The music started up again. A large man in black put his hand on the shoulder of the ranter. They walked out of the room together.

Carolyn turned back to Bonnie. She took a cleansing breath. It didn't work.

"Can't you help me?" she said.

"Go to the police," said Bonnie.

"I've told them what I know. They haven't helped at all."

"I can't do anything."

"No one believes I'm being followed."

"Maybe you aren't."

Carolyn's jaw dropped. "I'm not nuts."

"Okay, okay. Calm down."

Carolyn gripped the table. "I've been through enough and I want to know what happened here. If you won't talk to me, then I'll keep at everyone here until someone comes up with something that makes sense. I'm tired of running and I'm going to stop here."

Bonnie sat opposite Carolyn. "Okay, calm down. Let me think. The night before she was killed, Sharon left in a hurry. Usually she finished cleaning up then clocked out. That night she didn't and I heard about it the next night. It was my turn to lock up and I unloaded on her the night she died. I told the police the same thing, they didn't care other than to make sure it was Sharon I was talking about. Talk to Barlow, the bartender. I gotta go."

At the bar Carolyn got Barlows' attention.

"What can I get for you?" he said.

"Cola with ice." she said.

He sat the drink in front of her. "Two bucks."

"I'd like to talk with you for a minute," she said.

"You'll have to make it quick."

"I'm Sharon De LaFleur's roommate, Carolyn. Bonnie thought you might know something." She saw a puzzled look on his face.

"I didn't know she had a roommate." he said.

"Did she know anyone well? Who was her friend here?" she said.

"Why don't you ask the police about this stuff?"

"They won't talk to me."

"How do I know you're really her roommate?"

"You remember those earrings she wore? The feathery ones?"

"No."

"Well if you paid attention you'd know. I bought them for her when I moved in. They were a thank you gift for opening her apartment to me."

"So."

"She wore them most nights. I would think you'd notice."

"Look, maybe that's true. But I told the police what I knew about her. She pretty much kept to herself," he shrugged then started to wipe down the bar, there was nothing there, but he kept wiping.

"What about talking to people? Did she talk to you?" she asked.

"Not the night she died," he said. "She seemed in a hurry to finish up and took off pretty quickly, although if

I remember, now, she did the same thing the night before." He stopped wiping and looked thoughtful.

"Bonnie said the same thing. Did Sharon give a reason for leaving early?"

"That's what I mean," said Jim. "There was some urgency about leaving that night. She didn't normally do that. She tended to be predictable, done when everything was done…"

Carolyn leaned in. "What do you think it means?"

"Dunno. Maybe ask the guitar player, Jeffrey, he was asking about her earlier. He found her, you know."

"He did? How did he happen to run across her?"

"They live, lived in the same part of town." He nodded to Carolyn. "I've gotta get back to work now, OK? Talk to Jeffrey at the break." He left before she could reply.

Carolyn was getting the runaround. Nobody wanted to talk about Sharon. Maybe no one really knew her here either.

The piano player announced their last song before the break. It began with a languid introduction. Carolyn guessed it was a blues song. The guitar joined in. In the last hour, the patrons all seemed to have been switched out and a new set replaced them. Interrupted by the sound of silverware on plates, the music controlled the ebb and flow of conversation.

"What can I do for you?" said the voice next to her. Carolyn blinked and realized she had been day dreaming. The voice belonged to the guitar player. He held a tall glass with a clear liquid that bubbled up along the sides. Soda, she guessed. Up close he looked older than she had originally thought.

"You're Jeff?" she said.

"Jeffrey, officially. Jim Barlow said you were looking for me. Do I know you from somewhere?" He sat.

"No, you don't. I'm Carolyn Pendle, I was Sharon De LaFleur's roommate."

They shook hands, very formal, very polite. He had a warm, strong grip.

"I'm sorry she died," he said. "I didn't know her, really. I didn't even know she had a roommate. Is there something I can do?"

"I just wanted to know about her last few days. I think how she died is odd." She paused to gather her thoughts. "You found her that night, right?"

"Yes. I didn't even know it was her until later. It was dark and the police pushed me away as soon as they arrived."

What if this guy really was a killer? What if he had stalked her and then killed her on the way home?

"Were you involved with Sharon?" she said.

"No, not at all. Why?"

"The papers said you found her and the police suspect you."

"Of course. They've decided I'm the last person to see her. If you're going to accuse me of killing her then we're done." He stood up to go.

"Other stuff has happened. I've been attacked, the apartment was ransacked," she said.

"So tell the police."

"I did. They're busy."

"I'm the prime suspect. Did you know our drummer, Bill Clemons, died the other night?"

"What does that have to do with Sharon?" she said.

"He died here. I've been part of two deaths now."

"Do you think they're connected?"

"Of course."

"Why, of course?" Carolyn said. "What do Sharon and Bill Clemons have to do with each other?"

"Jim Barlow said Bill and Sharon dated. The police think I killed one or both of them out of jealousy."

"Did you?" She backed off a few steps.

"No." Jeffrey clenched his fists. "Bill was my friend. Why are you asking about all this anyway?"

"I told you I was attacked and the apartment ransacked. I also think I'm being followed."

"Why?"

"I think something happened here and whoever is after me thinks I got it. Whatever *it* is."

"You told the police this?"

"As though they would listen."

"I take it you're investigating this yourself, then?"

"I'm trying to find out why someone would be after me. So, yes, I am."

"Maybe I can help," he said.

"Maybe you should get a lawyer."

"Done. But he just tells me to lay low. I want to know about Bill."

"Are you sure? It may not be good."

"He was my friend."

"Then talk to me about Sharon," she said.

"Like what? I've followed the reports on TV and in the papers, but all they say is it's an ongoing investigation. I'm concerned the police are only looking at me."

He dropped his hands on the table. Carolyn could see lines around his eyes. Maybe they could work together.

"What if we pool our ignorance and try to figure this out," she asked. "You don't seem to be lying, and I'm running out of resources on my own."

"So go to the police, they'll help."

"They haven't yet," she said. "I've been attacked twice and got away. I've been hiding since the first attack. I don't want to end up in the news."

"What happened?"

"My apartment, our apartment was broken into. Sharon's stuff was ransacked. My things were gone through, but nothing was stolen. I don't know why someone wouldn't take something if they were simply robbing the place. They didn't. I checked. But I found some papers that were hidden in a book. I don't know exactly what they mean. It looks like they were here at the hotel at one point."

"What do you mean they were here?"

"The papers were stamped with 'Newsome Hotel' on them. Like a receipt."

He started to talk then stopped. He leaned in to Carolyn.

"I think you've found something that matters." He made a decision. "I need to finish the next set and close out the night," he said. "Can you wait around? It'll be twenty minutes."

"Okay," she said, "I'll wait."

Chapter Twenty

L ight from the computer screen reflected into Detective Madison's eyes. He squinted as he opened the autopsy report on William C. Clemons death. Clemons died of unknown causes and a tox screening had been ordered. The report noted that Clemons was healthy for his age. There was nothing in the bruises or scrapes from the fall that indicated previous injury. He had early onset arthritis, noticeable in his spine and shoulder joints. John scrolled through the rest of the report, didn't see anything that helped his investigation, so he clicked out.

"Just like the report on Sharon De LaFleur," he said to Officer Ferrin as she walked in.

"Detective," she said. "I don't know if this does much for your murder, but there was plenty of activity night before last at the Winsome Arms apartments. Where your vic lived."

"Which one, De LaFleur or Clemons?"

"De LaFleur," she said.

"What happened?"

Ferrin gave a rundown of the events.

"Good work," he said. "Was Green violent?"

"No more than expected. I think he's hiding something beyond the voyeur campaign," she said. "There was a break in at De LaFleur's apartment. Green said he saw another woman in the place. When we took a look around, there was evidence of someone having been there. But it was messy, drawers opened, furniture moved like the place had been ransacked."

"Did you get a name?"

"Green said it was Carolyn Pendle, not on the rental contract, a sublet. I found a credit card bill with her name and the apartment address. According to Green she moved in about six months ago. Has a job, but missing since the murder."

"I've got an APB out for her already."

"I also had the impression we just missed someone at the apartment. But Green said he hadn't seen lights in there last night."

"What about Green?"

"According to his rap sheet he was caught about ten years ago at the same game."

Madison slapped the desk and got up. "I think I'll have a chat with your Mr. Green. Seems like a man with a story."

Mr. Barry Green walked into the interview room and sat at the table. The fluorescent light buzzed and flickered intermittently. From the two-way mirror he looked haggard. Madison gathered up his papers and went into the room. Introductions were made and Madison began.

"According to your record, you've done this before. This time you'll end up with a longer sentence and time in the State system."

"I don't know what you're talking about."

"You're a peeping tom, a voyeur."

"Innocent until proven guilty."

"The evidence speaks for itself. You're in trouble and I can help."

"What do you mean you can help? You're a cop."

"I'm a homicide detective."

"I didn't kill anyone. What do you want with me?" He stood up. Madison stood up. They glared at each other. Then Madison sat, gesturing that Green should do so as well.

"I'm looking into Sharon De LaFleur's death. You showed me the apartment the other day."

"Now I remember. You picked up the glass."

"Yeah. And you told me you replaced the window pane in the door."

"What do I get?"

"For what?" Madison asked.

"You want some information about De LaFleur. I need something in return," said Green.

"That's up to the DA."

"There's gotta be a trade. Or I don't tell you anything."

"I know. All I can do is put in a good word depending on what you tell me. It'll carry weight."

"You're not giving me much."

"I don't know what you've got. Let's talk. You give me something solid I'll make an extra effort."

"Okay, I guess. It won't hurt."

"You showed me the kitchen after you fixed the window. What did it really look like when you went in to fix it?"

"I just went in to the kitchen. Glass all over. The chairs were knocked around, table was pulled away from the wall. That's all I saw."

"So what did you do besides fix the window?"

"Cleaned up the glass, put the chairs & table back."

"How did you know where they went?"

"They only fit that one place. And that's where they always were."

"So you've been in there before?"

Green slapped his hands to his head.

"We lifted your fingerprints throughout the apartment."

"What an idiot."

"Hmmm."

"Look, I didn't take anything."

"We'll find out about that as well. I want to know what the place looked like after Sharon De LaFleur was murdered. What did you really see?"

Rubbed his forehead and then spoke. "It was a mess. It looked like a quick but thorough search. Normally, if you're going through a place you automatically replace everything you touch."

"And you've done this before?"

"No, I . . . "

"I don't care. I just want to know about the De LaFleur apartment. Was the search focused?"

"What?"

"Did one room look more tore up than another?"

Green gained control of himself. "Probably the bedrooms were the worst. The drawers were almost empty. I put some stuff back and halfway closed them."

"Why?"

"It didn't look right. You can't leave things so messy. It was like amateur hour in there."

"Or maybe someone was angry."

"Yeah. Definitely."

"Anything else stand out?"

"A jewelry box was dumped on the bed."

"I would expect that."

"Yeah, but I don't think anything was taken. It was upside down and no stuff was scattered. Like it was tipped over and everything was left underneath it."

"Okay. So what did you get?"

"Nothing. They were too poor to have computers or anything. I looked in the tough broads room. No jewelry to speak of. The TV I was going to get later but other stuff happened."

"Did you ever see Carolyn Pendle there?"

"She the roommate? Nah, before De LaFleur was killed I didn't talk to them."

"Did you ever see anyone else there?"

"Nope."

"How about the last few days?"

"I don't think so. Wait a minute. The other night I thought I saw lights inside. I was up doing some viewing . . ."

"Binoculars?"

"Yeah. But I didn't hurt anyone."

"About the apartment."

"Right. There was a light that I thought went on, but it was only quickly, after midnight. I didn't see it again."

"Did you go into the place after that?"

"No."

Madison didn't believe him. "Green, if you want a good report you've got to tell me what you know."

"Why don't you stop asking questions? Isn't that enough?"

"You haven't given me any meat, Green. What are you forgetting?"

"Alright, alright. Let me think. Okay, I know. The last time I went in it looked like the books had been moved a lot. Every other visit, the books were untouched. Shelves were neat, spines lined up in perfect rows. This time they were a jumble. Some stacked flat. Sizes mixed up, a bunch pushed back to the wall."

"So it looks like someone wanted papers. Are you sure it wasn't like that after the window was broken?"

"Yeah, I'm sure. I've been in there enough to know what it looks like."

"How many times did you go into their place?"

Barry Green crossed his arms and didn't say anything. They stared at each other.

"I'll put in a good word for you," said Madison. He got up and went to the door.

"I don't want to go back," said Green.

"Don't do the crime."

In his office, Madison pulled up DMV info on Carolyn Pendle. Her driver's license was clean, not even recent change of address. An ATF search listed her as licensed to carry concealed with her current address at the apartment was the only one available. Madison made a request to look into financial records next. That would take time.

On a legal sheet he wrote out what he knew about the case so far. Two murders connected only by common work locations, both exhibiting no obvious cause of death. That meant that the tox report was vital. Two young people as victims, who aside from their working at the same place, have no personal association. An apartment incident that indicated someone's interest in Sharon De LaFleur hadn't been fulfilled with just the murder, it seemed to suggest the possibility that an object, drugs, money, or a valuable unknown was being sought. Or that coincidentally, a break in had occurred. Madison didn't believe in this sort of coincidence, so he needed to find the connection.

The disarray at the apartment revealed that not only had a search taken place, but that whatever was being looked for might not have been found since other events were still cropping up. Also, the missing roommate might be another victim or even be the perpetrator of at least one one crime. If he could find Carolyn Pendle, some of the questions might be answered, or new ones opened.

Madison felt the situation was a bit more topsy-turvy than he cared for. Usually suspects leaped out of the woodwork once the evidence was in. Some almost cried to be caught. Usually the list of suspects would eliminate false leads quickly. But not in this case so far. Like Alice falling into the rabbit hole, Madison thought there were too many odd, scrambled parts still showing up to lead him in the wrong direction. He saw bits that led somewhere, but the where and why fore were inconclusive.

Eddie scratched his scruffy face as he thought. There was no way he could go back to the Winsome Arms apartments now. He wondered if he should have torched the place. No matter. He sat brooding atop a cardboard box in the storage unit. He had taken some more earrings from the De LaFleur apartment on his last visit. He knew that was technically cheating, but earrings were nice tokens and it made him feel powerful. If they decided each set of earrings represented a victim, that was okay with him.

He got down to business. Surrounded by all this potential wealth, all the drugs that would get him out of here, he was relatively happy. Although he still couldn't seem to finish a simple burglary correctly. He'd traced the girl once, he could do it again. The roommate had gone to ground after the last attack so it would be more difficult. He would have to start from the Newsome this time. Not for her, but to find out if that damned receipt had really been picked up and was waiting to be used to nail him.

The girl would have to become secondary. He liked that, secondary. He wondered what they called the most important item. Not firstiary, but something like it. He was over his anger at missing the girl at the old house. He was over the fact that the wrong person had drunk the poison at the hotel. Who cared about a drummer anyway? He was even over the fact that it was taking so long to fix the mess that Sharon De LaFleur had put him in. Now he needed to focus. He needed to bring his will to bear on the chaos so life could continue as he had planned.

He was back to tracking down Jeffrey Grant. Grant had found De LaFleurs' body and Eddie could only assume the missing paper had been picked up by him. That meant Grant was now the only one left who could connect Eddie to the drugs. He would also need to be dealt with in the usual fashion.

Chapter Twenty One

Within two hours of Barry Green's lawyer paying bail and getting his release, he had sucked down three pints of the cheapest swill he could find at The Ace, his hangout. Dark, greasy, noisy with outdoor traffic leaking in through poorly constructed walls, Barry felt a camaraderie with the others who nursed their brews in the bar. If Barry were a sensitive soul, he would find his situation overwhelming. That wasn't his way.

With a fortified mind, he cruised out of The Ace for his next target. Out of the caretaking business, he sought to reclaim his dignity by fixing on his current problem, finding the missing renter from the De LaFleur apartment. It was her fault he had been arrested. Obviously she was the one wandering around in the dark apartment and playing games with the cops. He would find her himself and help her understand the situation he was in.

Barry wouldn't have identified the humiliation and anger he felt as the basis for his revenge, but his heart was bent. Bent toward getting back at that woman, that girl who had spoiled his whole set up. No more leisurely nights of beer and binoculars. No more respectful days of gardening and puttering around, fixing stuff at the apartments. No more naps in the basement tool room. He might as well be some cheap criminal looking for satisfaction as much as the retiring caretaker of his own domain. His thoughts wandered along like this as he made the walk to his apartment.

The notice on his front door from the management company gave him six days to vacate. His managers' keys had been confiscated when he was arrested. A look around his rooms showed most his tools had been lifted, he assumed someone in management had taken them, his weapons were confiscated, he couldn't even find a screwdriver to help get into De LaFleur's place and wait for the surviving member of the duo to return. After his arrest, he had wondered if Carolyn would return. She had caused him to get arrested, she was the reason for his trouble, and she would pay for butting in on his set up.

The rest of the day was spent packing his apartment into boxes. Fortunately he had a few knives in the kitchen, they had neglected to lift those, so he still had a weapon. A simple poke and slice with a knife and she wouldn't be a problem anymore. He worked out a plan that included breaking and entering, lots of waiting, and then an end to his troubles. Afterwards, he could head south and get lost in the crowd. Maybe Cabo Blancos. Maybe even stay in the states, just hidden somewhere. A big city would be fine.

The knock on the door echoed startled him. He waited a bit, went into the kitchen to find one of those knives and answered on the third knock. A burly figure in a maintenance style gray shirt filled the door. The name badge said Harry S.

"What do you want?" said Barry.

"Are you Barry?" said Harry.

"You kickin' me out so soon?"

"They decided to cut six days to one, tonight's it. You're out by nine."

Barry sized him up as below average intelligence, but above average muscle.

"Right. I'm packing now. Does that work for you?" He grinned.

Harry S. grabbed Green's shirt and pulled him close. His breath was stale.

"Yes. You've got two hours to finish up. I need you to come to the office with me. Paperwork and keys. I'll give you your check."

Unexpected, thought Barry. Harry released his hold on Green. The goon is gonna stay with me till the end he thought.

"I'll see you in two hours." As he slammed the door in Harry's face, he heard a voice through the door.

"I'll wait out here."

In the afternoon, Jeffrey and Carolyn met at the Riverside Cafe. He listened as Carolyn gave him a rundown of her situation.

"So how do you see this working out?" He licked the cream from the scone off his fingers.

"I don't have a place to stay right now, I'm camping out. Laying low. When I was attacked the other night after work I figured it was random, an accident. I was in the wrong place at the wrong time. That was before I even knew Sharon was dead. When I saw the apartment had been robbed and then I was hit again I didn't feel safe. Now I think someone was in there looking for something, but I don't know what."

"So you need a place to stay?" Jeffrey began.

"No, I'm not looking for a place. Camping out is fine, I do feel safe." She reached a hand across the table and placed it near Jeff's. "I'm just trying to figure out what happened. The police haven't come up with who attacked me as I ran home. And I don't think they've done anything about the break in at my place."

"So what do you want?"

"I've been thinking. We should work together; try to find out who killed Sharon."

Jeffrey sat back. He waited before he spoke. "You know I'm still a suspect? If we do work together you will become a suspect as well." He thought about Bill Clemons, he still hadn't been told what killed him, he may never know.

"I've thought about it. We both have little to lose, and I can't get into the Newsome without drawing attention."

"I think the two deaths are related. And I think they have something to do with the Newsome."

"I think so too. But I don't understand why I'm getting attacked or why the apartment was ransacked."

"Something important must be there. We have to figure out what."

"What if it's not about the Newsome directly? What if Sharon took something from there and brought it home? Whatever it is must be incriminating or at least embarrassing for someone. I think we need to go back to the apartment and take another look." She finished up her coffee and pulled out money to pay for the food.

"I've got to work until midnight," Jeffrey said. "Let me think about this teamwork idea. Meet me at the Newsome tonight and we'll decide what to do."

Rubbing his forehead with his fingers, Madison noted the time. It was getting close to seven and he wanted to wrap up the day. Nothing from the forensic report of the De LaFleur crime scene told him that a third party had been there. Nonetheless, he theorized that someone had been there and left no conclusive trace. Jeffrey Grant had a clean adult record and at this point Madison had no real reason to dip into the sealed juvenile case. His ex-wife had been interviewed in California and said he wasn't violent and she couldn't imagine him hurting anyone physically. It would have messed up his guitar hands and he was too vain to hurt himself like that. It turned out that she had fallen for a younger guy and left Grant after a long Acapulco vacation. It didn't work out. Now she was single.

Detective Marlin walked in with his raincoat on.

"Are you still burning the late night oil, huh?" Marlin said.

"I'm trying to get a bead on this stuff. Are you leaving already?"

"Done for the night." Marlin spun the visitor chair around and sat. He waited expectantly.

Madison gave up. "All right, what's the story? You've got something but I've got to ask, right?"

"It's not much, but I was looking over the crime scene photos from the apartment mess. Where your vic lived."

Madison nodded.

"Tucked in the report, it seems that the apartment had recently been broken into. Did you notice that?"

"Sure. Ferrin told me about it."

"Marks on the back door by the kitchen, general disarray in one of the bedrooms, looks like the vic's, and some unknown prints besides the ones Identified as belonging to De LaFleur and the ones that match Pendle."

"Okay."

"Forensic guys said it looked like a search had been done, but roughly. Not a regular burglary. Sure they looked in the usual places, but they also took apart cosmetics drawers and books. They also found partials around the kitchen window and on the night light in the vic's bedroom."

"I saw that. What are you thinking?" Madison said.

"Well, I looked at the report from the lab on Green's prints. He's eliminated. We see him outside the apartment, nothing inside."

"He told me he was inside. He even gave specifics," said Madison.

"Looks like someone wiped the place down after him. Remember all of De LaFleur and Pendle's prints were found on internal surfaces. In drawers and inside the jewelry box, the partials were external. And they are unmatched. They're not in the database." Marlin got up. "Hope I didn't mess up your night."

"I've got to think about this. So we have another actor." Madison grabbed his jacket. He and Marlin headed out the door. "Could you make sure I get copied on that report?"

"All ready copied it to you. The partials went through IAFIS with no hit."

They stepped out of the office into the cool, damp night. The rain had stopped and a breeze trickled through the leaves causing a symphony of whispering sounds to cascade into the night air as drops of moisture dripped leaf to leaf. The sounds of passing cars rose and faded, distant highway traffic kept up a steady hum in the background. Madison wondered where this case was going now.

Moonlight illuminated the Winsome Arms apartments. From across the street, Carolyn watched for activity in her own apartment. She pulled her sweatshirt close around her as the cool of the night settled in. Hopefully, Jeffrey would show up soon and they could do another sweep of the apartment. She had met him earlier at the Newsome and after more convincing he finally agreed to help. She knew he would. They decided to meet after going to home to change into comfortable clothes.

She hoped he wasn't helping her so he could get close. He was a nice guy, but he was too old for her.

She saw motion out of the corner of her eye. A dark figure was walking to her from down the block. She could barely hear his footsteps. As he drew near, she withdrew into the darkness. The scurrying of a squirrel through damp leaves startled the walker.

"Carolyn?" said the whispered voice. She could see him looking around. It was Jeffrey.

"Hi," she whispered.

"You scared me. I wasn't sure what you meant when you said to meet across the street." he poked his hands into his coat and waited.

"Let's get over to the apartment."

"Why are we sneaking in? It's your place," he said.

"Yes, but what if the guy is watching it still? If he thinks I've got whatever he's looking for then he might come back and make another attempt to get me."

"You really think so?"

"Yes. Now let's go."

Once in the apartment they went to De LaFleurs' bedroom. Using headlights Jeffrey provided, they took a systematic approach to the search. Starting at the door, they touched and moved every item along the wall, inspecting drawers in and out and under. Sharon had just a few sets of clothes. Lingerie for less than a week, enough socks and stockings for a few days of work, two sweatshirts, one set of sweatpants, even her closet held just one other set of work clothes and a few skirts and blouses. There were two dresses, dark colors, and several sweaters of wool and heavy cotton.

"You know, I don't think I recall ever seeing her go out," said Carolyn. She picked up a photo of Sharon on a beach. She was standing in the surf bundled up in a sweatshirt and shorts. Carolyn frowned at the picture. "She doesn't look happy. You know, I always figured she went out at night while I was working. But she was always home when I got here. I thought she went out and partied like everyone else. Maybe if I had gotten to know her better." Her voice trailed off.

"I'm not sure that would have helped." He swept his headlight around the room. "Look at this place, almost Spartan except for the books."

Carolyn went to the bookshelf. "They've been messed up by whoever searched here the first time." She picked up a book and flipped through it. Jeffrey came over and they began leafing through the books. Then Carolyn remembered. "You know I found a piece of paper here when I was cleaning up the other day. It was in one of the books, but I haven't figured out what it is." She thought for a moment. "Maybe that paper is what someone was looking for."

"What was on it?"

"It was a receipt or order sheet for chemicals. I figured it was something for the Newsome, cleaning solution or disinfectant."

"Do you still have it?"

"It's back at camp."

"I think we should look at it."

"Let's finish up going through the books. If there's nothing here then we'll take a look at the paper."

"That could be the key to figuring out what's going on."

"Or it could be nothing." Carolyn slammed a thick book into the bookcase. "I don't want to come back here again. Let's make sure now."

"Okay. Let's finish here." Jeffrey backed away. He began looking at books at the other side of the shelf.

"It doesn't make sense to think she'd hide something here when there is no place to keep it secret. She doesn't have a safe does she?" he said.

"Not that I'm aware of."

"What about in a vent or ceiling hatch? You see that all the time on TV and movies."

"This place is a closed environment. No open attic, the heat is electric baseboard, even the closet is build-it-yourself from a big box store."

"No storage? Not even in another place?"

"Not unless she rented a bin somewhere. I don't know about it."

They worked diligently and finished going through the shelves in De LaFleur's room and those in the living room. They found nothing.

"I know she didn't want me in her room, and I don't think she liked having to have a roommate, but she said they'd raised the rent twice in the last two years and she couldn't keep up."

Jeffrey pulled out his phone. "Three seventeen in the morning, it's later than I thought," he said. "Let's finish this, then go get some rest."

"All right..." her voice trailed off. "Did you hear that?"

"What?"

"It sounded like a door closing." She walked to the window and peered out. "I'm sure I heard a noise," she whispered. "I don't like it."

"Let's see what it is," said Jeffrey. He turned off his flashlight. Carolyn doused hers. They stayed close and crept from room to room. They heard the click of metal on metal in the kitchen. Jeffrey stepped into the doorway and then fell back onto Carolyn. She felt a punch land heavily on Jeffrey. She turned to see a boot come crashing down close to her face. The intruder was struggling with Jeffrey while she remained trapped under him. She freed her arm and grabbed the boot. The man fell over. Cursing, he kicked her and freed himself. Jeffrey rolled off of her and leapt at the man. He dropped him with a knee tackle and they fell heavily on the floor. The man released a leg and kicked Jeffrey in the chest. He scrambled up and ran out the door.

Carolyn jumped up and then felt pain along her side. His kick had connected better than she thought. She limped out the door and tried to see what direction he had gone. Across the street a van started up and tires screeched as it flew away. She was too far away to see the license plate.

"See him?" Jeffrey said from the doorway.

"It's a van. Maybe white. I couldn't see the plates."

"Damn," he said. "I hurt." He sat down in the doorway breathing heavily.

Carolyn watched him as he began to recover. "You need to see a doctor?"

"No. I should be okay. He came on fast and strong."

"It's the same guy that grabbed me earlier."

"Are you sure?"

"No. But it must be. There can't be that many burglars trying to get into this place."

Carolyn waited until Jeffrey could breathe again. They decided their injuries were superficial. The bruises would heal. No police for now. They both needed rest and would meet in the morning for breakfast.

"I'll walk you home," he said.

"No, I'll be fine. You need to baby yourself tonight. Not me."

"I'm not babying you."

"I can take care of myself," she said.

"Okay. I'm limping off. See you in the morning."

"I want to make sure you're close to home before I leave."

"You're going to baby me now?" he said.

"No, make sure you're safe."

"After I protected you back there?"

"After you fell on me? I don't consider that protection."

"It was the best I could do at the time."

"Right."

"I'm one block from here. You can go now."

"Which way?"

He pointed.

"Okay. See you at the Riverside." She took off at a jog away from his house.

Chapter Twenty Two

A streetlight flickered down the block. There was no frisson of romance between the two of them, but if this was how two people learned to become friends, then they were doing it. While Jeffrey wanted to get out of the suspect spotlight, Carolyn wanted to simply disappear into the woodwork and become invisible again. All of her interactions with people reminded her that she preferred to keep her people skills for rousting the college students and her personal time for herself.

As she arrived at the alley behind the house, she paused to get a look around. Her senses were out of sorts because of the late hour and her own frustration. If they hadn't been, she would have noticed the lights that flicked out and the motor that went silent a block away. She might even have heard the sound of a car door being closed. Carolyn found the path of rocks that led to the abandoned house across the swampy grasses. Silently she made her way into the house and collected the paper she had hidden away.

Inside the house, she clicked on a lamp. A quick survey of her food stores and Carolyn knew the mice had gnawed their way in, probably bypassing the traps she had laid. Everything edible was spoiled. Even the peanut butter jar with its hard plastic lid had been knocked over and Carolyn assumed the mice had gotten to it. Looking at the mattress and sleeping bag she could see seeds and a few other mouse signs. Her sanctuary had been breached and there was nothing she could do about it now.

A noise sounded behind her. A gloved fist knocked her off balance. She felt a heavy weight bearing down on her, throwing her across the sleeping bag and onto the floor. Guttural cursing and swearing close to her ear rang out. Her instinct for self-preservation kicked in and overrode panic as she rolled when the other body fell on her. She hit the floor with her shoulder. A fist pounded into her side, she couldn't think. A leg moved across her hip. Without thinking, she lifted her knee into her attackers' crotch. A growl erupted from him and he stopped hitting her. She opened her eyes and met his as the lamp crashed to the floor and rolled away.

Shadows danced around her now, she grabbed his ear and bit it. He yelled and pulled her hair. His gloves were bulky and kept him from getting the grip he wanted and she slid out from under. The smell of nervous sweat, her own or his, filled her nostrils as did the metallic odor of blood. An arm groped for her neck and the hard breathing close to her filled her with resolve. She picked up a wooden object, pushed away as she rolled and then slammed it into the attacker. She hit something soft, heard the sound of flesh being opened and felt the splatter of warm liquid hit her face. Another blow and then she rolled away and got up. The man screamed in pain and flailed his arms. One arm groping the air to grab her, the other covering the side of his face. She kept moving farther away.

Carolyn stumbled over a bag, grabbed the canvas tent that surrounded the room and jerked it down onto the man. Her hiding spot was blown.

The invectives of the man grew more repetitive and less inventive. He was close to getting untangled from the canvas. Carolyn leaped across the mess of the room, grabbed a towel, and then stomped on the lamp. The darkness was sudden and startling. She picked her way out of the house and ran through the tall grass and mud. Down the alley into the next street and then quickly crisscrossing the next few blocks, she finally slowed down. At the sound of cars approaching, Carolyn ducked into doorways and stayed in the shadows. Once she thought a slow moving van was stalking her, but it turned down a side street and disappeared.

Now what, she thought. Her plan had been to lie low until this was over, then get back to her normal life, a safe, boring, secure life. Her plan had been to figure out what really happened to her roommate and then move on. Whoever had attacked her was crazy. Maybe she should go to the police and tell them what she knew. But what exactly did she know? Nothing. By now Carolyn had wandered into Hendricks Park. It was the haunt of transients and other night crawlers. Through the trees she saw tents set up in a clearing, there were no lights. Night sounds filled the air.

She could hear the rushing of water from a nearby creek and realized that the heavy fog and mist from earlier hadn't lifted but was hanging in. She was surprised she could see the tents in the clearing, though they were just outlines. She also began to notice that she was a little sore from the hits she had taken. Her shoulder was aching more and more as she walked. If she hadn't been so tired she might have begun to enjoy her victory over her attacker. She didn't know if it was the same guy as before. It could have been. It probably was. She stopped and sat down at a picnic table, she slowed her breathing, her hands propped up her head. The quiet enveloped her, natures' sounds receded into the background, fatigue dropped onto her like a warm quilted blanket, her eyes closed and she fell into oblivion.

"Hey, you gotta get up, lady!" The old guy was bent over shouting at Carolyn.

"The kids are racing through, they'll rob ya!"

She heard the words but thought they were part of a dream. Or maybe they *were* part of a dream and she hadn't really heard the words. She didn't know any kids, just college students. Why would someone want her to wake up now anyway, it wasn't time. Then she began to remember.

"What'd you say?" She sat up. She could smell rancid fruit and a foul closeness like spoiled grains wafting around him. An old army coat shades darker than normal hovered near her. His tousled hair stuck out from under a blue gray watch cap. Dirty finger tips poked out of his gloves, a black plastic bag was slung over his shoulder.

"Who are you?" she said.

"Don't matter," he said, "Just tellin' ya to get up an away. The kid's 'll get what you've got and leave ya with nuthin'." He rambled away.

"Got it," she said. "I'm moving." She stood and felt achy from sleeping on a bench. Moving her damaged shoulder sent sharp shocks through her. After taking a few steps she loosened up and distributed the aches to other places. Motion seemed to help a little. She made her way down to the creek and washed up. The cold water did not feel good. As her fingertips began to chill, she dried her hands on her pants and heard the sounds of young voices drawing near.

The fog had lifted and the footfalls of stampeding youth became sharper. They were approaching en masse from the main path through the park. She retreated deeper into the clumps of brush that dotted the hillside park. A rash of brambles would have to protect her while the animals passed through. She had heard about the marauding groups who picked on the vagrants but had never seen them at work. A glance at her phone told her the day was under way if you counted six in the morning daytime. Carolyn found what looked like a path and squeezed further into the brush to conceal herself. She felt relatively safe.

Plodding feet thumped by, bits and tats of ragged singing moved closer along with the burps and blats of testosterone on parade. Unable to see through the brush, she thought it was only three or four boys terrorizing the park. They shouted slogans of hate harshly punctuated with curses. One of the ruffians carried a stick and beat it on whatever was close. She could hear concrete being whacked, bushes attacked, and the whack of stick against tree as they drew close.

Concentrating on being relaxed while holding still took more effort than it should have. She was exhausted from the events of the previous day and now felt the effects in her inability to concentrate. A flush of spasms tore through her. She could smell stale beer and the sweet stench of pot. Then the wind shifted and the odors drifted away. Sharp voices berated each other loudly and their cursing faded into the distance.

Carolyn was holding her breath. She breathed out. By the time the noises subsided, she had squirmed her way out of the brush and felt safe enough to move around. Morning already and it was time to prepare for her meeting with Jeffrey and possibly an end to her self-imposed exile.

She managed to finish up her morning ablutions and felt somewhat reconciled to risking another trip to her apartment for clothes to replace those she left back at the picnic table where she had slept. At close to ten, she seated herself on the edge of a decorative planter across the street from the Riverside Cafe. Carolyn spotted Jeffrey as he approached from the south. She crossed the street and they met near the Cafe door.

"What happened to you? I thought you were going home."

"I got to the house and the guy was there. I was totally surprised, lucky I got out."

"Are you okay? Do you need to see a doctor?"

"I think I'm all right, my shoulder got whacked pretty well when he fell on me, but I can move it. No doctor right now, no money." She whispered the next words. "I think the guy who attacked me is probably the one who killed Sharon. Otherwise, I don't know why else I'd have been followed and attacked."

"Let's get you some food," he said.

After ordering breakfast they talked over recent events.

"As far as I know, the police don't know about me. I don't want to become the focus of an investigation especially if it's going to waste time on me. They need to focus on the guy who followed me," Carolyn said.

"I get that, but you've got to keep the police in the loop. You may know something they need. That guy knows where you live. He may have even followed you here."

There weren't too many people in the cafe this morning. Most had gone on to their work or shopping. Up against the far corner by the kitchen entrance, a television mounted high on the wall made an abrupt switch from a local gardening show to a news report. A red ribbon across the bottom of the screen reported "Live news: fire at abandoned house." Camera shots of flames curling around the eaves of a roof line, a stream of water arcing onto the window of a front room, a crew of fire fighters unrolling hoses and getting into position all told the silent story of a local disaster. Jeffrey saw it. He was about to comment to Carolyn but she was staring up at the screen.

"What?" he said.

"That's my place. That was my place. He torched the house."

"What about your stuff, should we get over there?"

"No. I had nothing I can't do without."

A waitress pointed a remote at the screen and turned up the volume.

Carolyn dropped her head and closed her eyes. She sighed deeply.

Jeffrey waited. He was drawn again to the events on the TV. The house was set apart, in an untended field. The neighborhood didn't look upscale, but wasn't thoroughly neglected. The blaze was being controlled by the fire fighters. While hoses were set out, there was no hurry to get the water trained on the house. They were pouring it on the weeds and debris in the yard. A reporter came on who explained the decision to let the fire burn. The caption at the scene said the property was derelict, the owner had been contacted, they had decided to let it burn and would watch it for safety purposes and to control the blaze. The fire had been reported by neighbors two hours earlier, no one was seen in the area and prior to the fire it was an eyesore to the people who lived nearby.

"So now what?" he said. "Do you have another place to stay?"

She shook her head. Her shoulders slumped and her head dropped.

"The stuff I grabbed was all I had," she said. She covered her face with her hands.

"I've got a room, a second bedroom. If you want it, it's yours," he said.

Carolyn breathed deeply. She removed her hands and sat up. She watched the television news showing the fire on the screen.

"Maybe for now. Until this works itself out," she said.

"I think you need to go to the police. You need to at least let them know you are alive."

"I know. I don't want to."

They finished their breakfast. On the sidewalk outside, Jeffrey listened to Carolyn. She began to unburden herself to him.

"I thought I was safe, but the guy still found me. I've never been scared like this before. When I grew up, my family was not friendly with local cops. My dad drank too much. He got caught driving drunk over and over. He spent lots of nights in the back of cop cars going off to the drunk tank. Eventually his DUI history caught up with him and he went away for a few years after an accident that put a kid in the hospital. Mom told us he wasn't coming home. When he did show up again, he didn't stay. He was defeated, down all the time. Mom would yell at him." She was pacing as she spoke.

"He loafed around town, couldn't hold a job, and then he died. My brother, Dan, became my mentor while Dad was still alive. We would escape to hiking trails or camping trips on weekends, just to get away and relieve the pressure on Mom. After Dad died, Mom collapsed and withdrew. My brother finished high school, worked lots of odd jobs. Then Mom died. All the while, I thought we might finally settle down. I finished high school and started college. Within a year Dan got sick, cancer. He died in January of my first year in college. It seems like a long time ago, it was only five years. After a year or so I heard from the state treasury department that the house had been sold to pay back taxes."

"The leftover money, it wasn't much, they gave it to me. I was able to finish college with it. I've been on my own since then, a little money saved up, but I've always felt out of the mainstream. Not antisocial, just comfortable in my own skin. Maybe it's made me selfish. I just don't want all that stuff made public, hashed out on the TV or in the papers."

"That's a hard time to go through," said Jeffrey. "My offer still stands. And I still think we need to bring in the police. You're being hunted down. They've got me pegged as a suspect and you may be able to clear that up."

"Maybe."

"Why do you think he burned the house down anyway?"

"I guess to get me moving. Perhaps even to make me more desperate. I don't know where he's going with all this."

A taxi drove by. Two women in business suits were across the street talking and a UPS truck sat near the corner where a man was unloading boxes from a van to another business with a hand truck. The mist from earlier had abated and the temperature had dropped. Not quite chilly, the wet asphalt made the sound of cars passing by swish like a Doppler effect between the brick faced businesses of downtown. At times the effect was disorienting as the echoes seemed to come from multiple directions as they moved through.

Chapter Twenty Three

Madison settled down at his desk as he read through the report on Carolyn Pendle. No record, no traffic problems; seemingly, no family as well. She had fair grades through college, no assets worth mentioning. His phone rang.

"Madison." He closed his eyes and waited until the Chief asked her question.

"Nothing conclusive on the ME report. I'm sure you read it. We're pursuing the connections to the Newsome Hotel. Something will break. I hope it's soon."

He listened for a moment. Officer Arkin stepped into the cubicle. Arkin grabbed a note pad, scratched a message, tore it off the pad and slid it to Madison. As he left the room he signaled a phone call with his hand to his ear then disappeared down the hall.

John made a few perfunctory sounds into the phone as he listened. He picked up the note paper and read: 'Talk to me about the fire.'

"I've got the situation. I'll let you know what I know when I know it," he said.

He hung up the phone. He didn't need political pressure to close this case. He needed evidence that pointed to someone credible for the murder. At this point nothing convinced Madison that the guitar player had a reason to kill De LaFleur. The missing roommate had more incentive simply because she was missing. Not a great reason to murder someone. Finding her would help, even if it just eliminated her as the perp. Maybe Arkin's news would break the case open and solve it. He chuckled to himself and realized he was nearing that point in the case where grasping at straws was almost respectable.

Madison thought it was unusual that Arkin would be around this late in the morning. Arkin worked the graveyard shift by choice and should be asleep by now. He walked down the hall, refilled his cup, then made his way to the officers arena, the bullpen, the corral, whatever they were calling it these days.

Madison walked to Arkin's cubicle. He could see him plugging away at a computer. Next to the keyboard lay an open incident report book containing his handwritten notes. Madison noted the slump of Arkin's shoulders. It was late, the guy was tired.

"You got something for me, Arkin?" he said.

"You see the blaze from the house fire last night?" Arkin asked.

"Sure. It's front page news in the paper."

"I picked up fire security after they doused the house the first time. They let it burn down but it didn't burn all the way through. The forensics guys were called in when the marshal called the fire suspicious. The place was lived in, probably campers, but the name 'Pendle' showed up on a book under some stuff. You'll probably see it in the fire report, but they won't get to it for a day or two. The preliminary won't have it. Pendle is the name of the roommate in the De LaFleur case, right?"

"Yes, it is," said Madison. "Good catch. Who's running that one at the fire department?"

"Don't know. I just talked with Bill Ren who was finishing up his report on site. They were gathering pictures and he pointed that one out. I told him I'd get the info to you."

Madison thought Arkin was sharp, good with details and seemed to get along with other departments pretty well. He'll go places in a short time, he thought. "Thanks. I'll get his report, any other things you see on site?"

"No, it was too dark, but I'm sure the pictures will show quite a bit. That's all I've got for you now. I've got to finish and get out of here. If anything else comes up, I'll get back to you, okay?"

"Get some rest." As he walked away he wondered what to make of that information. Was she just crashing there? Did some homeless person pick the book up from somewhere? What or who made the house burn? What did this clear up, other than the fact that Carolyn Pendle had been there?

Back at his desk, Madison picked up the phone just in time to hear a voice, "That's a pretty quick response, John. I didn't even hear it ring through."

"It didn't, I just picked up to make a call. What's on your mind, DeBrough?"

"Your Carolyn Pendle suspect has been seen with the other suspect, Jeffrey Grant. They were down at the Riverside Cafe. They got breakfast and spent quite a while talking. They perked up when the house fire showed up on the news. The call in came from a beat officer. They left half an hour ago."

"That doesn't make sense. Why were they together?" Madison said.

"Want me to get a statement?"

"I'll take care of it. We can pick her up and get some questions answered."

Madison sat back in the chair. Now what, he thought. Why are Pendle and Grant together? If Pendle's hiding place is burned down, are they working together? He called the officer in charge.

"I need you to pick up Carolyn Pendle and Jeffrey Grant. Get their information from the De LaFleur murder file. We've got photos for Grant and for Pendle. They were last seen together downtown by the Riverside Cafe." He paused and listened for a while. "That's it. Right away."

Was this the break that he needed to wrap up this case, or a merely a diversion?

By three that afternoon, Jeffrey and Carolyn had made their way toward Hendricks Park and were close to Jeffrey's home. Carolyn was determined not to go back to the apartment. She now saw that it was too risky. She would have to rely on an ATM and her existing savings to get by.

They were walking through a light drizzle that made their footsteps sound juicy with an echo off the concrete sidewalk, the tires of cars passing by sizzled through the water.

"Once you get settled at my place, we need to go to the police," Jeffrey said.

"I know. I heard you before. Weren't you listening to me?"

"You've had a tough time. It won't get easier. Especially with your options for hiding being eliminated."

"Give me time to think." She stopped walking and turned away.

"You don't have it. They'll be looking for you for sure now if they haven't been before."

"I hate going to the police."

Jeffrey was imperturbable. "With the fire at the house and the report that's going to be out, I don't think you have a choice."

"It would be nice to figure this out before I have to talk with them."

They walked silently for a few minutes. Jeffrey spoke first.

"I want to talk to them before going to the Newsome tonight."

"Okay," Carolyn said.

As Jeffrey and Carolyn walked they were being watched. A block behind them a white cargo van moved slowly along the street. It stopped at times and idled. As Jeffrey and Carolyn would turn a corner, the van would arrive, stop and then idle once again. Deep in their own thoughts, neither Jeffrey nor Carolyn noticed. A light drizzle began, cool but not cold, and the dampness sharpened the sound of their footsteps.

As they walked up to Jeffrey's apartment, the cargo van rounded the corner and parked. Jeffrey let Carolyn enter first and then followed. He locked the door, then standing back from the window he stared back at the cargo van down the street. He could see exhaust drifting from the tailpipe of the vehicle and dissipate in the air.

"Where's the light?" said Carolyn.

"Just a minute, I want to check something," said Jeffrey. He watched the van pull away from the corner. As it passed under the streetlight, Jeffrey strained to see the driver. All he could make out was a silhouette. He thought that it was a man. It was too quick, too dark, and too blurred through the rain to tell for sure. He flipped on the light switch.

"I think we were followed," he said.

She glanced out the window.

"He's gone already. A white van, stopped back at the last corner."

"You don't suppose it was a coincidence?"

"Not likely, once we got inside he waited just long enough to see we were in then took off."

"Should we leave now?"

"Something tells me we've got a little time."

"What do you mean?"

"I don't know if this is the guy who did the house fire. I don't know if we really are in danger or if we're being followed to be intimidated. This just isn't the way it happens on TV or the movies."

"Should we call the police?"

"I can't read the license plate," he said.

"If this is the guy after me, this could give the police something to go on."

"I've got that detective's card somewhere," He dropped it on the counter. "Detective John Madison," he read.

Jeffrey made the call. He heard the phone ring through and then switch to a phone tree. He punched in Madison's extension. He expected a machine and got a voice.

"Madison here."

"This is Jeffrey Grant. You interviewed me about the De LaFleur death and Bill Clemons death as well."

"Grant? I've got people out looking for you now. Where are you?"

"Home and I think I was followed."

"Why do you think that?"

"This cargo van pulled up at the corner as I opened my door, sat for less than a minute, then took off."

"Did you get a plate number, a make?"

"It's a dirty white van with those double doors on the sides and back."

"So why do you think it was following you?"

"I told you it sat in front of the apartment then took off when I looked out at it."

"Okay, are you home now? Can I use this number to get back to you?"

"Yes, I'm home. The number is my cell."

"We need to have a conversation here at the station. I'm sending someone over to pick you up."

"I've got to get to work. Can we talk after the job?"

"This is a murder case. It won't be a long conversation. I need to see you tonight."

"Okay, then. I'll wait for your car."

When she overheard Jeffrey's reply she sat down on the couch and exhaled.

"So why is Madison sending a car?" she asked.

"He's got more questions. I can't tell if he believes me about the van."

"I'm not going with you," she said.

"This would be the time to tell him what you know."

"It's not the right time."

"Do you want an invitation?"

"I don't know if it will make a difference."

"An invitation?"

"No. Telling him what I know. It's not much. It doesn't seem like anything." She got up and began pacing around the living room. "If we were followed here and the guy sees you taken away by the police, maybe he'll assume you're under arrest and clear out."

"But if he was following us, then he knows you're here as well," said Jeffrey.

"You're right. There is a back way out, right?"

"Yes. So what will you do?"

"You're going to end up at the Newsome, right?"

"After meeting with Madison, sure."

"So I'll meet you there tonight. I'll clean up here and then go out the back."

"Okay. Let me get you the spare key."

"Fine."

When Jeffrey returned from the kitchen there was a knock at the door. He handed her the key.

She watched him open the door and then leave with a patrolman. She walked from the dark kitchen into an equally dark living room. If the man who followed them was outside she didn't want to let him know she was still there by putting on the lights. It could also be that she was getting paranoid. She needed to clean up after sleeping outdoors last night. Getting clean always seemed to help. Then she would decide for herself if talking to the police was really the best policy.

Chapter Twenty Four

Jeffrey rode silently in the car with the patrolman. He was either going to jail, he thought, or he was going to be let go. It had to be one or the other. He let his thoughts wander as they rode along.

What had he forgotten to tell Carolyn? He hadn't taken time to tell her where to find things in the apartment. She would have to forage. Then he wondered what he had left out that she might find. He remembered that on the guest bed were photo albums from college. A while back he'd begun digging out old photos from his college years and using them as inspiration for some new music he was writing. The photos brought back memories of his early days in the music business.

He had started out as a teacher of composition, but not successfully. Then he gave private lessons to rich kids in L.A. He worked as a songwriter on the side at the time, but fell on his face. Married and overworked, he finally admitted defeat. She left him, he quit teaching, limped by on pick-up jobs at weddings and private parties for a year, and finally hooked a cruise ship gig that gave him a year out of town and steady work. He found his mojo again on a weary Sunday morning as the S.S. Windtracker plowed through Caribbean waters. Restless in spite of the late night gig and soured on the general ennui of another cruise heading to another port, he would never forget the morning he stumbled onto the deck.

As he walked among the hungover passengers sleeping under the stars, he heard voices, untrained and unmelodious, he thought, but voices singing a Capella. Down in the ships' chapel he took a seat in the back of the room and listened to the songs and a homily that touched his heart. It wasn't profound, the speaker obviously wasn't a trained professional, but he was moved nonetheless. After a few more cruises, he gave up the floating gigs and moved to North Glendon. Away from his old stomping grounds in California he hoped to find balance in his life. He began teaching again, then worked his way into the jazz community. Bill Clemons and Harmon Webb became a trio when Jeffrey booked the jazz gig at the Newsome Hotel. That was then.

"You haven't told me everything you know," said Madison. He slammed the door as he walked to the chair in the interview room.

"Hi," said Jeffrey.

"You're impeding my investigation, Grant. I don't know what you are up to but it doesn't look good."

"What are you talking about?"

"Who did you meet at the Riverside today?"

"A friend. Why?"

"Does that friend happen to be a person we're looking for?"

"How would I know?"

"Conspiring to commit a murder and withholding evidence from a felony." Madison slammed his fist against the table.

"What are you talking about?" Jeffrey rose to his feet.

"Sit down, Grant." Madison matched him standing up. "Now."

"Give me a clue."

"You were seen. I've got a BOLO out for you and your girlfriend."

"Girlfriend?" They both sat.

There was a knock at the door and Korman stepped in. He handed a file to Madison then left.

Madison took a look at the papers inside then walked out of the room.

"Korman, what does this mean? Do you know what this drug is?"

Korman shook his head. "This one's new to me. I've seen variations on crack and meth and heroin, but not this stuff."

"Orthenadrine citrate." He picked up his phone and dialed the morgue. "You're still there? I figured I would leave a message and get you in the morning."

"No rest for the wicked," said Dr. Winslow.

"I'm looking at the final tox for De LaFleur and see orphenadrine citrate. What are we looking at?"

"Norflex or Flexon, it's used for muscle pain. It's prescription. I haven't read the report yet, I'll get to it in the morning."

"Would you see if the lab found that in the Clemons screening also? I haven't heard from them yet, but it might connect the cases."

"Sure. Is the morning okay for you?"

"Yes, should be fine. Thanks, Jeane. Are you done for the day?"

"I'm just walking out."

"Not me." Madison hung up the phone. He read through the report thoroughly.

"So what is this stuff?" said Korman.

"Prescription medicine. Can you find out what this actually does to someone? Dr. Winslow said it's used for muscle pain. And see if it was found in the De LaFleur apartment."

"Got it."

"So what does this add to my talk with Grant?" he said to himself. He closed the folder and walked back into the interview room. Opposite the door, Grant stood looking into the mirror.

"Grant, you've been holding out. I need to know about your relationship with Carolyn Pendle."

"She came to me a day ago at the Newsome."

"Why?"

"She's been followed and even attacked by someone."

"I know about the break in at the apartment. Then Pendle disappeared. She's on my short list of suspects."

"Then you also know she was hiding out because whoever broke in has made more attempts to get to her."

"She didn't report anything."

"For whatever reason, she doesn't feel like she's being taken seriously."

"She could be the one who killed her roommate."

"Or not. Innocent until proven guilty is the phrase I've heard."

"Statistically it's someone the victim knows."

"Someone burned down the house she was hiding in."

"I know. That's how we discovered she was still around." Madison sat at the table again. Jeffrey walked over and sat opposite Madison. "The fire looks like arson."

"Carolyn wouldn't have burned her hideout."

"You seem pretty sure for someone meeting her so recently."

"She wants to find out who's stalking her. She called the policewoman who took the first report but didn't get a reply. She's independent and doesn't trust authority much."

"Where is she now?"

"I don't know."

"Where did she go after the Riverside?"

Jeffrey shifted uncomfortably. "We went to my apartment."

"Is she there now?"

"No. We were followed. That's why I called you. She said she didn't want to stay knowing the van followed us."

"The mysterious cargo van?"

"It was there."

"What can you tell me about it?" said Madison.

"What I said on the phone."

"Think. Give me colors, size, type of plate."

"Let me think. It was dark. It was a white van, not like those ones that are high off the ground. It was industrial looking, a few years old with no side windows."

"I knew you had something. What about the plate, local, another state?"

"Local, in state, I think. I recall letters but no numbers."

"A name or acronym?"

"No. Letters at the beginning. Three. Then a space then something else."

"Next time get a license plate number, take a picture."

"Next time I may not have a choice. If that's the killer he knows Carolyn and I know each other."

"So he will stay away. Two against one are not good odds."

"Or he could be getting desperate."

Madison picked up the folder and stood up to leave. "I don't know what to believe from you, Jeffrey. Right now I'm letting you go. Don't leave town. If you see Pendle again I want to know about it. Call me."

Chapter Twenty Five

She walked up to the desk. A uniformed officer waited for her.

"I've never been here before. Where would I find Detective Madison?" she said.

"And you are?" said desk Sergeant Riggs.

"Carolyn Pendle."

"Let me make a call."

They sat in an interview room. Pendle was across from Madison.

"I've been looking for you," said Madison.

"I thought you might be," she said.

"Where have you been hiding?"

"I've been moving around."

"You get attacked, a house is burnt down, your roommate is murdered, and then you evade the police. What are you hiding?"

"I've been afraid. It's not normal for me to run. And I'm not even sure what I'm supposed to do."

"Most people would ask for help right away. Now that you're here, what was your relationship with Sharon De LaFleur?"

"We were simply roommates. We barely talked. She was quiet."

"So why not make yourself available to be interviewed sooner?"

"I've got issues with people in power." She rubbed her hands together as though trying to warm them. "Look, this isn't about me. I picked up a paper at the apartment the other day and I wondered if it has anything to do with Sharon's death."

"Let me see it."

"I can't figure it out." She handed the folded receipt to Madison.

He read it then got up and walked out of the room. He picked up his phone and dialed.

"Korman, I've got a receipt for drugs. The signature looks like it might be Stone. Get me one of the forensic team to pull prints off it. I'm in the interview room."

He sat down opposite Pendle. "Why didn't you get this to me sooner? You could have saved yourself and your boyfriend some trouble."

"I've been running a lot." She drew in a deep breath and exhaled. Her shoulders fell and it looked like she was relaxed.

"I know. You were seen."

"I don't have a boyfriend."

"What about Jeffrey Grant? You were seen together at the Riverside Cafe."

"He's helping me out."

"Do you know what the receipt is for?"

She shook her head. "Looks like medical stuff to me."

He leaned close to her. "It's for the drug that killed Sharon De LaFleur and likely killed William Clemons. Where exactly did you get it?"

"It was stuck in one of Sharon's books. I was cleaning up a little after the apartment was broken into."

"You'd never seen it before?"

"No."

"So why did you keep it?"

"It was unusual. I just slipped it in my wallet."

There was a knock on the door and a forensic tech walked in. Madison pointed to the paper laying on the table. She put on latex gloves and picked up the paper with tweezers then dropped it in a paper folder. Madison signed a receipt and the tech left the room.

"Where are you staying now?" said Madison.

"Jeffrey offered me a place until I can sort things out. Am I going to be arrested?"

"Not now. I will need to talk with you later so keep me informed about where you'll be. There will be more questions as we verify your information."

"So I can go?"

"Yes. We will talk soon."

When he got back to the apartment Carolyn wasn't there. It was close to time for him to go to the Jazz Room. Shortly after dusk, Jeffrey pulled his scooter out of the back shed. It was a BMS Palazzo, 150cc with a small trunk stuck on the back. He strapped his awkward-to-carry guitar case onto his back.

The employee lot next to the hotel's back door meant he didn't have to use the main entrance. Jeffrey locked the scooter to the metal fence post and the picked up his gear.

"Who's your partner, Jeff?" asked Oliver. The clerk was lounging against the registration desk and grinned as Jeffrey entered the lobby from the service hall.

"What are you talking about?" he asked.

"She's in the Jazz Room. She's been here for a while, very patient. And she's very young."

"Just a friend," Jeffrey said. "Is Clark in?"

"He left for the day, you know managers don't hang around longer than necessary."

"I need to talk to him. You have his number?"

"Clark isn't available until eight tonight, dinner date with some corporate types."

"Okay. You have a number I can call after eight?"

"Not my shift, but it's on the list by the desk, left side."

"I'll call him later." In the Jazz Room, dim lights and the emergency signs barely illuminated the room. Carolyn sat in a chair by the main door. She gestured to Jeffrey that she had heard him talking. They made their way over to the lockers behind the stage and Jeffrey switched on the lights.

"I didn't want to talk in the open, but the fewer people know we're here, the better," he said. "Oliver won't talk unless I tell him."

"Who's Clark?"

"He's the hotel manager. I think we should stay here, Clark can comp me a room. I can't afford to run away and my place isn't safe right now."

He could see her thinking about it.

"This will be safe and anonymous," he said. "If the manager gives me a room, I'll play for a night gratis. I don't know if he will go for it, but I want to try."

"What happened with Madison?" she said.

Jeffrey told her about the interview.

"It looks like either the police or the stalker is going to get me," she said.

"You need to go to the police. They're looking for you and probably watching me. I think Madison is tough but fair."

"Okay. I'll go in the morning. I want to be sure."

Madison finished off the lukewarm coffee. It wasn't helping keep him alert anymore. Another late night and he was still chasing down scraps of information. He picked up the phone.

"Sergeant, Madison here. I need someone to run a search on the DMV database. I'm looking for a late model, white cargo van. Probably used for deliveries of medical or chemical supplies. Keep it within fifty miles of town. No identifying logos so probably licensed to an individual." He listened for a while. "I know. It's a potshot but I've got to start somewhere. Let me know when something shows up."

He thought about the medical findings. Flexon or Norflex didn't sound like a common drug. Specialized drugs like this were rare and easier to trace, he hoped. He needed to know more.

"This is Madison," he said after the message recording started. "What would this Flexon be used for specifically? How soon would it affect someone taking it? Are we looking at pharmacies or clinics or hospitals as users? I know you won't get to this until the morning so call when you've got something. Thanks, Winslow. I owe you."

In spite of the hour, Madison finally felt like these traces of evidence might be leading somewhere constructive. He still didn't see where, but it felt right. If the drug trace was specific enough and the DMV search led to a small enough group of vans, then he might be getting close to the perp. He wasn't so sure that Grant killed Sharon De LaFleur now. So much evidence pointed elsewhere.

"I can get some cash if we need it. Do you still want to figure this thing out or do you want to get away from here?" said Carolyn.

"Bill Clemons was a friend and I knew Sharon, they shouldn't be discarded. Besides, I don't like being followed."

Harmon Webb entered the room and brushed by Jeffrey. He wore his street clothes and headed straight for his locker.

"So what's on for tonight, Jeffrey?"

"Webb. This is a friend who will be sticking around tonight. Carolyn."

Carolyn started to move over to shake hands.

"Piano player, I don't do handshakes."

Carolyn sat back down and stared at Harmon Webb. Jeffrey shrugged and motioned for her to wait. He grabbed his clothes from the locker and headed for the changing rooms.

"Webb's a little peculiar, but he's okay," he whispered as he walked by.

"I heard that," Webb said.

"I know," said Jeffrey. The door slammed behind him.

"Are you a relative or something? You're too young to be his girlfriend, right?"

"I'm a friend. We have, had, a mutual acquaintance. I'm staying with him for a little while."

"Musician?"

"Security."

"Security what?"

"I work security at the University."

"Sounds risky to me, music is safer."

"Jeffrey's helping me take care of some business. Personal stuff about our friend."

"Well, then I won't ask." Harmon grabbed his own clothes from the locker and headed into the changing rooms. She was tired, fidgety, feeling overwhelmed by what was going on. Being with Jeffrey Grant wasn't all that reassuring. Why had she have agreed to stick with him anyway? He wasn't her boss, wasn't her father. He didn't know what to do either. He couldn't even be sure he could help her if the bad guy found her.

It could have been someone Sharon dated, but the only one she had ever met was the drummer guy, Bill. At the time Sharon hadn't mentioned that Bill was the drummer at the Newsome. Even that had been at least a year ago.

As she sat and waited it felt like time was catching up with her. She thought about the loss of her stuff in the fire. It wasn't much, clothes and camping gear, but it was a big blow. Stripped of her possessions, cut off from her apartment, separated from even the few friends she knew from work. It felt like too much. She felt tired, then empty, and now anger began welling up inside.

Jeffrey walked out and saw Carolyn across the room. He could swear she was talking to herself. Eyes closed, hands clenched on her knees, her breath going in and out in controlled puffs. He thought she looked like a kettle about to blow over.

"Now what?" Jeffrey asked.

"It's just too much. Like I'm going to explode and cry and scream."

"Go ahead, I've been yelled at by the best. Musicians are notoriously angry. Supposedly it's for the art, but mostly they're just immature."

"Not me."

"Probably not, but whatever is getting to you won't be going away soon. If you want to vent, go ahead, I really can listen. My ex thought I was a good listener."

"It's just that even the shallow resemblance of routine, of a pattern that is normal has been blown away. I thought I had some control over my life, a job, simple as it is, no real friends, but an income that could lead to some sense of security. Now everything is gone. No place to live. I can't even get my stuff from the apartment. I don't think it's safe. Just a few days ago, life was safe. I knew my own routine. Family is gone, has been for too long already. Now I don't even know if I'll keep the memories, I may have already lost them."

She slumped her shoulders, unclenched her hands. Being verbal loosened her up, like breathing slowly in and out. Jeffrey watched her slowly straighten up and take control again.

"You're doing well right now." He walked over and sat next to her. "I think now is a good time to just be in this moment. When we figure out who is after you, us; then we'll have the luxury of looking around and getting our act together. Right now is one of those *in the moment* times. Just hang in, be alert, it looks like we're learning enough to really bother someone. I just don't know who, yet."

"I'm still angry from his attack at the house."

Jeffrey put an arm around Carolyn and waited. The dressing room door opened quickly and Harmon Webb burst through.

"What are you love-birds up to?" he said. "Let's get to work, you guys can make out later, I need this job to get through the week and pay off the mortgage." He shook his head and left the room. Jeffrey thought he heard a chuffing sound as Harmon walked away. Jeffrey glanced at his watch.

"We can make out later." He followed Harmon out.

"That's not happening," she said.

"I know, but it is funny. Come on out and get a table near the stage when you're ready. I still think we should keep each other in sight."

Chapter Twenty Six

B arry Green was disappointed. The jail cell smelled like urine was leeching out of the walls. It stung his nose. He remembered too well the last time he had been prison. When he got out last time he said he would never go back. Here he was. He despised the person he had become.

His promise to himself had dissipated. He was weak. He began slamming his fists into his head. The sound was a dull, fleshy thudding. Afterwards, he stared into the distance contemplating his future. Once again he was behind bars. Once again he was dead to the world.

He should have protected himself. As he thought back over the recent past the smells in the jail disappeared. He paid no attention to the idiotic buzz of the light in the ceiling. He stopped hearing the cries and screams echoing from around the ward where others complained and random shrieks filled the air.

His 'aha' moment welled up from within. The scales dropped from his eyes and madness rushed in to find a place to stay. It truly wasn't his fault he was back in here. No, others were manipulating the events and he knew that that wretched woman was at the base of it all. Until he invaded her space, he had been free.

Guards Malloy and Feliz consulted the chart and made notes on the clipboard. The cell doors were open and a few of the men lingered near the round picnic tables with fixed seats that dotted the open area in the west wing of the prison. On three sides of the open room were double rows of cell doors. Each door led to a room with two beds, a sink and toilet, and a small table permanently attached to the wall. Worn paint was the order of the day everywhere. Gray, red, and green were the industrial colors favored by the city for this particular facility. Today was clean out day.

Although late, Barry was sure it was his turn to make the ride to county lock up. He couldn't remember if he had been to court yet. He wasn't even sure at this point what he had been convicted of, but he was positive the steps he heard were for him.

Clamoring up the metal steps, Feliz stopped at the top.

"Green, Barry," barked Feliz. "Get your stuff."

"Why?" said Barry. He didn't move.

"You're out of here. Furloughed. Too crowded and we've got some nasty boys who need to take your spot. Get your goods and come on, you've got paperwork."

The white cargo van stopped in the unloading zone. It backed into a slot and stopped inches from the raised platform dock. The man in the uniform opened the side doors, pulled out the hand truck, and stacked boxes onto the cart. He checked a clipboard, shoved it onto the top of the stack, and pushed the cart into the freight entrance of the Newsome Hotel. His delivery included cleaning supplies for the hotel, and then a stop at the cafe/lounge. The last time he had delivered here, Bill Clemons suffered his fatal attack.

Tonight he would leave his mark on another member of the band. The one who was getting too close to him. The one who was also harboring the girl who could identify him. He would have preferred to find out where the girl was, but he was too concerned about being traced to try to speak with the guy. That was the disadvantage of working solo. Who could he trust? No one, not a single person he knew would be able to keep quiet. He worked solo.

At the bar, the delivery man left two boxes on the counter near the espresso machine. A short conversation with the barista, mostly 'yes' and 'no' and 'what will you need next' followed. He left with the cart. Within five minutes he returned, this time his jacket and hat had been removed, the dark jacket replaced by a gray cardigan with pockets. He didn't look too different, but he was less obviously the delivery guy. He seated himself near the entrance. In the darkness of the room, with candlelight as the main source of illumination, he could survey the room pretty much unobserved. He watched as the musicians assembled on the small stage across the room. They were the focal point with two small overhead lights that glowed soft yellow. Light strips lined the small stage along the floor. A few tables had dinner guests, mostly couples enjoying a late meal and hoping to catch live music as well. Sitting quietly, the man had blown out the candle on the table and slid it close to the wall.

He planned in his head the best way to accomplish his mission and eliminate the guitar player. He kept his hand in the cardigan pocket and fingered the needle he had earlier prepared with the Flexon.

"I've narrowed the van down to six possibilities," said DeBrough.

"That's pretty good," said Madison. He rubbed his eyes. There were dark rings around them. "Get Korman and track them down. I think we're close on this one."

"Okay. He's on his way in."

"Remember, we're looking at independent contractors." Madison reached across the desk for his coffee. Empty again.

Dave Brubeck's "Take Five" started off the nights' set. Jeffrey and Harmon knit their sound together. Instinctively, they filled in the spots where the percussion would have jumped in. They traded off leads and let the music flow, making the bridge between melody and chorus smooth. There were no rough passages, Jeffrey and Harmon were focused solely on getting the music to sound right tonight.

Hearing the group for the first time, a newcomer wouldn't have noticed the lack of percussion. Within an hour a light crowd had filtered in from the hotel. A trickle of couples came in from the street entrance and as the night grew dark outside, transitioning from blue to black with a trace of sodium orange dotting the sidewalks down the street, the evening settled into another glorious night at the Newsome Hotel.

Tinkling glasses, hurried waiters, candles flickering, jazz tickling customers' ears all contributed to a mélange of sound as light dinners were served and drinks passed around the room. An undercurrent of energy moved through the room and peaked in different places at different times, like a lake buffeted by winds that twist and turn their point of origin and sporadic white caps form then disappear.

The temperature rose in the room as the night wore on. He unbuttoned his cardigan. He had left the evidence of his crimes at the Newsome and they had been picked up by the young woman whom he had disposed of. Where had she put it? He had searched her apartment thoroughly, there was nothing there. She might have even tossed the evidence out not knowing what it was. But his suspicions were that the papers had been picked up, most likely by the nosy roommate whom he couldn't find because of the interference of the lousy guitarist. He was now more vulnerable than he had ever been and knew he had to stop just a few more people to be safe. The sickly roommate of De LaFleur was key. He'd lost sight of her because of the guitar player and would soon take him out of the way so he could wrap up the whole problem. He had to admit he'd fallen down on the job. He had left himself open to being seen. His operation was in jeopardy and now he had to spend his time fixing things. Now he would have to leave the area and rebuild. He cursed his luck and remembered that he was waiting once again for a chance to resolve the problems his own sloppiness had created.

Madison picked up the phone.

"We've got a van owned by a dead man," said Korman.

"What?"

"Cargo van owned by Christopher Stone fits the description. Christopher Stone died thirty years ago. DMV shows a false address for the van. If it existed it would be on the train tracks downtown by the post office."

"Let's get street patrols looking for the van. Concentrate on two locations, the apartment complex where the action has been and the Newsome Hotel."

"Got it."

Madison thought about the new information. If the guy was looking to recover his paperwork, then those two places were obvious. He would probably keep to his routine so no one would suspect. He would also be asking question of people he might not normally talk with. He would be the new guy.

At the counter of the Newsome, Jim Barlow looked for the signal to get another coffee for the man who delivered supplies to the hotel. Between glances around the room and keeping an eye on orders for the night, Barlow felt tension hanging over the evening. Jim glanced over to the man in the cardigan and saw the signal, a small nod and a finger pointed at the coffee cup.

"When does the first break come up?" said the man in the cardigan. "The band. When do they take a break?"

"Another fifteen minutes and they stop for ten," said Barlow.

"Good music, buy them a round on me."

"Sure. You know them?"

"Nope." The man stared at the stage. The conversation was apparently over. Jim made a note on a napkin as he walked back to the bar. He stuck it to the polished steel front of the drinks fridge.

A smooth rendition of "Time After Time" began playing. Jeffrey laid out the rhythm while Harmon Webb played a variation of the Sinatra version. They made the sounds blend and the lack of percussion didn't hurt the overall tone of the song. By the time both of them had traded off solos, been through the melody several times and then finished off with a soaring crescendo the room had felt the energy and almost convulsed. After the song ended, Barlow saw Jeffrey take off his guitar. Jeffrey walked to a table where a woman sat alone.

"We're breaking now," Jeffrey said. "Do you want something?" Carolyn looked smaller as he stood waiting. Small not because she shrunk into herself, but small as though she was uncomfortable. Not dressed for an evening out, she didn't really fit into the room.

"I'd like one of those fruit and salad dishes." She pulled her hands off the tabletop and tucked them under her legs. A small smile crept across her face and suddenly Jeffrey could see why he liked her. When she smiled it made him smile.

"How much is it?" she said.

"It's on the house," he said.

At the counter, Barlow caught Jeffrey's eye as he walked toward him. Jeffrey lifted his hand and gestured for a drink. Barlow pulled a glass from the rack. Jeffrey place Carolyn's order with one of the servers. When he got to the bar he saw his club soda sitting there. Barlow had added in a sprig of mint.

"Fancy drink for a musician," Jeffrey said.

"The guy sitting at the stool bought a round for you guys. When someone buys you get the works."

"Don't tell me the invisible man stopped by?" he said.

"Weird," Jim said, "he was just here, you know, the delivery guy that doesn't talk. Said to buy a round and put it on his bill. Look, he dropped the cash and must have left just now." Barlow collected the bills and then rang it up at the till.

"I've got a fan tonight to entertain," said Jeffrey.

"I saw you stop and talk to her. A bit young for you isn't she?"

"If she were my date. Yes. She's a friend who needs help."

"Sure she is," Barlow said.

"You know, they knocked down our pay after Bill died. A hundred bucks a night less, not a third but still not a great move for us. I don't think we can look for another drummer anytime soon." Jeffrey noticed the time on the clock. "Tell the guy thanks for the drinks the next time you see him. I've got to get back."

Jeffrey sat down at Carolyn's table. "I've got a feeling this is the night when something big happens with Sharon and Bill's murders. Have you ever had that sort of feeling? It's not anything definite, just a vague sense of change about to take place."

"I think it's only because we were being followed earlier."

"I think this is where it all began and is where it's all going to finish."

"You guys are playing well. If I didn't know better I would have thought you were always a duet, not a trio."

"You should have heard Bill Clemons. He didn't just keep time. He was a musical drummer. Bill could really lie back when the music needed it. His instincts for accents and dynamics were spot on. He wasn't obvious, he really filled the song out and made it work." He took a sip of his soda and then glanced at his watch.

"Time already?" she asked.

"Yes," he glanced around the room. "Second set is mostly up-tempo. Harmon really likes this one, it's his, I'll back him up, but he gets the air time." He smiled at Carolyn.

Chapter Twenty Seven

After getting released, Barry Green had walked to the nearest bar. A few drinks later he decided to get back at Sharon De LaFleurs' roommate. She had caused his problems, she would pay. He remembered that De LaFleur had worked at the Newsome. He thought he would see if the roommate worked there as well.

Green walked into the lobby of the hotel. He clenched his fists in the pockets of his jacket. There was tension in his face and in his darting eyes. He didn't know where he was headed, but he knew it was here somewhere. From the lobby he could see too many doorways. There were too many places for little rooms that people could hide in. Tonight he was chasing, someone else would need to be running, tonight he had the momentum and everyone else would need to catch up to him. No more running for Barry Green.

He spotted an electric sign across the lobby. "Cafe and lounge" sounded like a place to look. He mumbled incoherently to himself and walked into the Jazz Room. Obviously out of place, his dirty jeans, holey tee shirt, and off season wind breaker set him up for some odd stares and questionable looks from the wait staff and a few of the patrons. No one approached him, but the glances cued him in that his anonymity was blown.

Too bright to hide, too dark to see faces in the room, he thought. He walked to the bar sat down and nodded to the bartender. "Give me Jack, double, and keep the bottle close."

"This is a coffee bar, no straight drinks, sir," said Barlow.

"What? No wonder I don't know about this place. So what do I do?"

"I can get you whiskey in coffee, or a hot toddy, a variety of other drinks. Here's a menu."

"Nine bucks?" Barry breathed quickly in and out. Gotta keep my head, he thought. Gotta stay cool. Don't draw attention. Keep it cool. He closed his eyes then took a look through his wallet. He couldn't stay here long.

"Give me the coffee with Jack," he said. He'd have to make a loop around the room and see if she was here. He got up, tossed a ten onto the counter and began a slow walk around the room.

It was an old ballroom. The walls were dark wood and met a high ceiling that faded into blackness. It had deep mottled carpet that felt like expensive luxury. The candles that dotted the tables barely illuminated the patrons. Barry wanted to step up to each table and scrutinize the patrons. He couldn't do it, no way someone wouldn't get upset, be offended, and strike out at him. It was what he didn't need. Stay low key and get out of the light. He still hadn't decided exactly what to do to her once he had her. He'd come up with something. He was good with spontaneity sometimes.

Jeffrey glanced over to Harmon Webb and gave the lead to him, the ivories bounced with joy as Harmon cut in with a tribute to Tin Pan Alley. Conversations at the nearby tables drifted up and down. Jeffrey wondered if anyone heard them. Sometimes it seemed the music was only background noise to the conversations. He kept glancing over to the table where Carolyn waited.

Most of the people at the tables were here for desserts and finishing out their night on the town. Some came to sober up before heading home. Jeffrey, Harmon, and Bill knew that, accepted it, enjoyed the laid back atmosphere that let them play the music they loved and not feel under a great deal of pressure to perform. Jeffrey's instincts told him that tonight was different. He saw the guy at the bar get up and start moving among the tables. The man seemed to be wandering. This could be trouble, he thought.

From her vantage point, Carolyn noticed the form moving along the far wall. The man seemed to be stopping, looking, and then moving along. He was taking his time. She knew he was looking for her. It was the guy. She blew out the candle at the table. If he was struggling with the light, then she would help. She leaned over to the next table and extinguished the candle there as well. She wouldn't make it easy for him.

She heard the sound of the guitar going out of time from the piano. Up on the stage Jeffrey curled down into himself. He tilted forward in the chair as though taking an extended bow. Carolyn thought he would fall off the stage and instinctively got up to go help him. Harmon stopped playing and watched Jeffrey fall forward.

The silence, then the crash on the stage drew everyone's attention. People got up and went to the stage to help. Harmon reached Jeffrey first, extracted the guitar, and laid him out flat. Jeffrey's breathing was labored. Carolyn reached Jeffrey. She leaned in close and listened as Jeffrey spoke to her.

Barry Green watched the hustle on stage and then saw the woman he was looking for. She was helping the guitar guy. He wanted to charge down there and pummel her. He wanted to run away and get stone drunk and forget. He found an empty table and sat, keeping his eyes on the stage.

An older woman in a dark suit pushed her way through the crowd. She grabbed Jeffrey's wrist with one hand and waited.

"I'm a doctor," said the older woman. She told Harmon to call 911.

Groggy, as though drunk, Jeffrey said, "Carolyn, go to Barlow, at the bar. He'll stay with you."

The doctor held him down with one hand and gestured to her partner with the other. He handed her his phone after dialing someone. She began talking into the phone. Jeffrey grabbed her arm.

"I saw the guy, my drink," he said, then he convulsed. He grabbed his stomach and pain crossed his face.

Carolyn didn't want to leave but knew she couldn't help. She felt like someone was staring at her. She moved quickly bashing her legs and knees against chairs as she headed toward the bar. The sound of her own breath accelerated, urgency enveloped her. A flash of cold shocked her, her heart felt too loud in her ears. She pushed aside the tables and people between her and the bar. She could see Jim Barlow ahead standing frozen with his hands flat on the counter.

Barlow tried to remember what he was supposed to do but his body wasn't responding to his brain. He remembered that Jeffrey had told him about needing to watch over Carolyn, but he hadn't really been listening. The girl was stumbling toward him through the tables and chairs across the room, Barlow saw a man rise out of a seat on the other side of the room. The chaos created by Jeffrey's fall infected the room. People seemed to come alive. Some were wading up to the stage, some calling 911. Carolyn arrived at the counter about the time Barlow finally went into action. He pointed to the exit and told her to meet him at the door. He picked up the short bat from behind the bar. The heft of the bat felt pretty good in his hand. The man Barlow had noticed was getting close. He was obviously following Carolyn. The man didn't see Jim.

Barry was close to his quarry but shocked by the man approaching quickly with the bat. He ducked and felt a glancing blow hit his back. He dropped to one knee and then propelled himself up while the bar man began to swing down at him. He grabbed the wrist of the man and punched him at the same time as he stopped the club. They slammed into the edge of the counter, toppled several chairs and crashed to the floor.

A man in a gray cardigan grabbed Carolyn and pulled her to the door.

People had noticed the scuffle. Someone screamed. A man shouted to stop. The man with the cardigan pulled Carolyn roughly as she struggled.

Barry Green and Jim Barlow separated for a moment. They lunged at the man with Carolyn. In the struggle the man in the cardigan stuffed his hand into the pocket and pulled out the syringe. Half empty, the plunger popped off as the man groped it and felt it stab into the flesh by his thumb. Barry and Barlow subdued him quickly and Carolyn twisted free and headed for the door. She was met by Officer Jane Ferrin and Officer William Hernandez. Ferrin pushed her to the side and told her to stay. She and her partner jumped into the scuffle and began cuffing the men.

Madison and DeBrough and Korman arrived along with the EMS team. The melee subsided as guests streamed out of the room. On the floor lay Barry Green, Jim Barlow, and Eddie Delmar. They were cuffed with plastic ties and ready for interrogation.

Chapter Twenty Eight

Detective Madison adjusted his tie and paced. At the gray metal table sat a middle aged man, scruffy under the fluorescent light. His thinning dishwater hair was cut short. He sat back in the metal chair and stared at a point in space. His arms were crossed and his feet were flat on the ground. The only information he had given Madison was his name, Christopher Stone. Records from the driver's license were clean.

"Mr. Stone. Why were you trying to kidnap Carolyn Pendle?" said Madison.

"Who says I was?" said Stone.

"She does. As do all the witnesses at the Newsome. What's your story?"

"No story from me. It was all a mistake. I was rescuing the girl. She was in trouble from the other guy."

"And who is the other guy?"

"Never met him."

"We found the needle in your pocket."

"Needle for what?"

"That you used to spike Jeffrey Grants' drink."

"Who's that?"

Madison slammed his fist to the table. He ran his hand through his hair and took off his jacket.

"I don't know what your game is Mr. Stone, but I will find out."

"You don't have a reason for holding me here."

"You are a suspect in two murders and an attempted murder."

"I want a lawyer."

Madison paced the hall outside the interview room. A public defender had been called and was on the way. Korman and DeBrough were walking toward him.

"Two things, Madison," said DeBrough. "Christopher Stone is one hundred thirty-two years old according to the census bureau. He died in 'seventy-two."

"Our guy in there is Edward T. Delmar according to the partial fingerprint we found on the syringe," said Korman. "He's a local who delivers medical and housekeeping chemicals for hotels and hospitals. Under Christopher Stone he has a clean record with the DMV. According to the map, he lives on the railroad tracks near the Post Office."

"Under the name Edward Delmar," said DeBrough, "he lives in the old part of town on Harrison. His expired driving record is littered with infractions."

"Any convictions?" said Madison.

"Nothing. He's kept under the radar," said Korman.

"So what's his story then?" said Madison. He walked back into the interview room. The public defender startled when Madison entered. He shuffled papers into a folder.

"Do you have charges to press on Mr. Stone, Detective?" said the attorney.

"Not Mr. Stone. No."

"Then he's free to go."

"I will be charging Mr. Delmar with two murders though, as soon as the DA gets the paperwork ready."

"Mr. Delmar?"

"Your client. Edward T. Delmar."

Delmar swore and leaped out of the chair at Madison. After he was subdued by an Officer and Madison, he sat cuffed at the table.

"Mr. Delmar. You left prints on the syringe."

"So what."

"So we're getting a search warrant for your home on Harrison. We're also getting a warrant to search your cargo van."

"Go ahead. I'll be out in another forty-eight hours and you won't have found anything to connect me to your crimes. Murders or whatever you say they are." He gestured to Madison with his cuffed hands. "I don't need these things anymore. I'm in control now."

"I doubt that." Madison frowned. "Why the subterfuge, why two identities?"

"You know that. You've seen the DMV records."

"Who cares about a few tickets? Those don't exempt you from driving especially if you're not CDL. Local delivery isn't regulated by anyone except the people you drive for."

"I wanted a new identity. I don't like Eddie for a name."

Madison didn't believe it. He had to probe another direction. He leaned in close to Delmar. "I think you're a sick bastard who killed once for necessity then liked it. I think you're hooked on deciding who lives and dies."

Madison watched Delmar's face register a smile then become neutral. He had hit a vein. Delmar was hiding a darker secret than he had imagined. He left the interview room and called Korman.

"I think this guy has a history beyond the two murders. I don't know why, but I feel like he's good at hiding. He's good at redirecting you to another target. Did you see what he did when I suggested he likes killing?"

"He smiled," said Korman.

"Let me know when you are ready to execute the warrant at his house. I want to be there."

Early the next morning, Carolyn entered the hospital room where Jeffrey lay. Through the hospital window, the morning light cast a blue tint over the room. Carolyn could see Jeffrey staring out the window.

"You okay?" he asked.

"Better than you are," she replied. "I only have a few scratches and bruises from last night. What about you?"

"The doctor said I was poisoned by orphenadrine citrate. Some sort of muscle relaxer that could have killed me. Fortunately it was a low dose I shouldn't have any problems. For being a muscle relaxer I sure feel bad."

"It was probably the fall. Good thing that doctor was there."

"Detective Madison said they suspected the seltzer water was drugged, it's being tested."

"He was here? When did he come in?"

"Early. He had questions and I couldn't sleep."

"One of the guys was from my apartment complex. What was he doing?"

"Madison said Green blamed you for his being fired. He's back in jail."

"Who was the guy who grabbed me then?"

"I don't know. Madison said they were holding him for the murders. Jim Barlow told Madison the guy delivered supplies and cleaning chemicals to the Newsome. By the way, Barlow got stitched up and sprained a shoulder. He's in a sling."

"Why did the guy try to poison you anyway?"

"Madison wasn't sure yet, he thought it had something to do with both De LaFleur and Clemons. They found the same poison in both of them."

"After Madison questioned me last night, I went back up to the hotel room. They wouldn't let me come to the hospital and stay."

"Good. At least the room got used. I should be getting out of here this afternoon," he said.

Korman took an inventory of the items from Eddie's pockets. A key stamped with a number and storage facility name led them to a location on the south side of town. Madison, Korman and DeBrough presented the warrant to the manager and were directed to a unit with an outside entrance.

"It's the old part of the place. First and only building with an entrance I can't see from the office," said Harold Fineman. He spoke and walked quickly.

"Been here long?" asked Madison.

"I started just after retirement. About twelve years ago. This job keeps me out of the bars at night."

"What about this unit. When did the occupant start using it?"

"Maybe six years ago. I can get dates from the records. I didn't see the guy much, but I knew his van when he drove in."

"Van?"

"One of those generic white cargo things. When people key through the front gate we snap a picture for security. He's got a sticker on the back of the mirror from the same college I went to."

They rounded a corner and Fineman went right to the number 278. He brought the bolt cutter up to the lock.

"Can I see that paper again?" he asked.

"I can cut it if you want. This is a murder investigation."

"Got it." The tool sliced neatly through the padlock and dropped to the ground.

Before them was an eight by ten room of boxes stacked almost to the ceiling.

"Gloves on," said Madison. "DeBrough, see where the CSI unit is. They need to document this."

"I've got them on the phone. They just arrived."

"Tell them to key in 5432 and they can drive back here," said Fineman. "Looks like someone's in a heap o trouble."

In minutes the team arrived and pictures were taken. They taped off the area and began cataloging the contents.

"This looks interesting," said a young man at the back of the room.

Madison joined him. The man opened the shoebox with the earrings. Another box held a bottle of Flexon. In the next week, the investigation made connections to a series of thefts and subsequent sales of Flexon and other prescription drugs to pharmacies, usually small, local establishments that received cut rate prices. Orders were placed directly with Eddie and he provided official looking receipts for his clients. As far as the clients knew, the drugs and prices were legitimate. Small quantities, low overhead, and all profit for the entrepreneur Eddie had become.

"No sugar for me," said Carolyn. She settled back into the sofa.

Jeffrey brought out the tray with cups and tea.

"Are you back at the apartment?" he asked.

"Yes, for now. The rent is still beyond my pay grade. I'll start looking soon."

"I'm glad you came by."

"You look like you've recovered well."

"I'm fine, I still ache at times but that will go away."

"Did you ever find out the whole story on Eddie Delmar?"

"Just what the papers said. It seems he stabbed himself with the drug during the fight at the Newsome. It didn't kill him, but he did collapse after talking with Madison at the station."

"I thought he died."

"He did. He was killed the first day in prison at County. One of the inmates knew Bill Clemons and knifed him."

"Madison told me the paper I found was a receipt for the drug. But why would he kill for that?" she said.

"It was a stupid mistake on his part, he probably left it at the Newsome one night and then realized Sharon had picked it up. Why she picked it up, no one knows. He must have thought it would tie him of the theft of the drugs."

"But Madison told me he didn't think the paper would necessarily have led them to him based on so little information."

"I think a certain amount of paranoia goes with being a crook."

They sat in silence and listened to the drizzle of water as it glanced over the gutters outside. Overcast but not dreary, the rain was falling late in the day and a vestige of sunlight hinted at the coming of spring. New rain, fresh rain, it all added up to a season of light that everyone in the town of North Glendon waited for.

No one knew exactly what this spring would bring, usually rain, but perhaps this year was different, there could be less rain, more blue sky and precious sun. Maybe global warming was giving this region a new lease on life. Maybe the days ahead were brighter and more hopeful than the winter gone by. Maybe.

ABOUT THE AUTHOR

M Roy Duffield lives in Oregon with his wife. They have two adult children. After thirty years as a video editor in New York City, he returned to the Pacific Northwest to pursue writing interests. In the interim, he worked as the film editor on a feature film, "Moonhair: A Bow and Arrow Fantasy."

He is currently working on the first in a series of private detective mysteries based in the Pacific Northwest. An avid family man and hacker golfer, he is adamant about continuing to hone his craft while enjoying the benefits of a relaxed lifestyle in the west.

Visit his website at www.MRoyDuffield.com.

Made in the USA
Middletown, DE
28 September 2015